KEEP THE GHOST

SCOTT KELLY

ISBN-13: 978-1514289426
ISBN-10: 1514289423

Cover by Greg Poszywak

Also by Scott:

[sic] (2013)
The Blue (2014)

www.ScottKellyWritesBooks.com

Contents

1. Lacuna

THE DEAD DON'T DIE. Death is something a living person suffers through, once the dead are gone from here. The departed don't know anything about dread, or longing, or the inevitable. They leave that to the survivors.

Kayla wants to give everyone her death, and I'm supposed to help.

A damp wind blows in from the gulf, and I catch the storm front in my teeth. The world is dark blue, in the tones of a sunrise swathed in wet clouds.

"You don't have to do this," I remind her. "A lot of people are going to miss you."

"Yeah, well, I'm not one of them." Kayla's mouth moves independent of the rest of her, which is otherwise focused on a cell phone. She clutches it with both hands, pale face squinting into its blue glow.

She stands on a long arc of South Texas coast that stretches into the oblivion of low light. Salt-born spears of tough gulf shrubs rise behind her, clawing at the sky. The land is half swamp, half shell-covered sand, a primal place defying any postcard expectation of what a beach should be.

The phone tips down, and she glares over it. "If you would mind your own business, you wouldn't be worrying about me now."

This is true. Still, I found a duffel bag full of money in Kayla's room—how could I not ask her about that?

"You need to allow for human curiosity," I explain. "And hide your shit better."

Gray waves roll over the tops of her pink water shoes, depositing sand between the laces. While her thumbs twitch over the keys, she speaks: "Just help me siphon the gas." Then she looks beyond the phone again, eyes meeting mine for a moment. "Please."

1

I walk to the trailer and climb on it, using the jet ski's handlebar as leverage. Once up, I crouch, so that my face is even with the little watercraft's tank. Waves tug at my legs, sucking the sandals from my feet, draining out between my toes. Cold.

When the clear plastic tubing drops into the tank, I blow on the other end. My breath hits resistance, bubbles to the surface. I suck hard on the tube then pull my mouth away, and gasoline spills into the Gulf of Mexico below. The little cloud of rainbow pollution is drained away by the falling tide.

Gradually, the stream slows to a trickle. The jet ski is empty, or close to it. I pull out the tube and toss it into the bay.

"You know what to do, right?" she asks. The phone is gone, and instead she holds her waist-length brown braid. The eyeliner streaks down her cheeks—black tears for a dark day.

"I know," I reply. I almost tell her not to go again, but then reconsider. I've told her a dozen times, begged her to think about it, about her parents, about what I'll have to do. But, here I am. Things will only be worse if I don't help. "Be careful. Make sure and call me."

Kayla pulls a neon blue life jacket across her chest, buckling the lowest of three straps first, then working upward. "I'll be fine," she says with a quaking voice. "I just need to kill my shadow."

"It's still dark," I remind her. "It's all shadow."

The last clasp snaps shut. "This is when they talk."

"I don't think you understand how light works," I say.

"It's a metaphor, dumbass. Use your brain." Kayla turns her head to watch a pelican as it takes flight from a fern-shrouded pond, beating big wings against the sky before gliding over the bay.

She pulls a dark gray duffel bag from the dry part of the beach and dusts small shells from the bottom before peering inside. Stacks of twenty dollar bills, bundled with rubber bands and stuffed inside plastic bags. In goes the cell phone she's been using—a cheap, disposable thing I've never seen her with before. Her smartphone is in the truck, where it will stay. That can't follow her across the gulf.

Kayla rifles through her satchel, ensuring the seals are tight on the waterproof bags. Satisfied, she zips it up, then swings the duffel bag over her shoulder. With one hand on the grip, she lifts a leg over the jet ski's seat. She twists the key and pushes the start button.

Kayla is really going through with this.

But, nothing happens. She tries again, and again, nothing. And then Kayla is staring at me, this panic in her eyes, and I'm a stupid boy doing the same thing I always do when a girl looks at me that way—I help her. The key isn't all the way in, so I jam it down with my palm. I twist, then push the starter. The jet ski rumbles to life, and I step down.

I turn the crank on the trailer, and the watercraft lowers into the bay until it floats, and is lifted gently clear by a wave.

"Now you can go kill yourself," I say, trying to smile.

A seizured curve grips her lips—she's also trying to smile. It doesn't work.

"You guys are going to miss me so much. See you at my funeral."

Kayla revs the motor, running the jet ski on what little fuel is left in the lines and at the bottom of the tank. She rides away, bouncing over the white-foamed tips of the chop. I watch until she disappears into the gulf.

Staring at my phone doesn't make it ring. Neither does holding it in both hands, squeezing it, or shaking it. Kayla is supposed to call, to let me know she's made it to the other side.

Except she's not calling, and I'm losing my mind. We didn't plan for this. It's been four hours. Four hours of pacing the beach and staring at the horizon for any sign of her. Four hours of almost calling the police, or her parents.

I stare out at the bay one last time, hoping to catch some glimpse of her on the water, hoping maybe she'll change her mind and come back. Hoping I can avoid the next step.

But it's not happening. It's been too long; she could be in trouble, trapped between worlds.

I turn back to her red truck, let myself in. I sit on the seat with the door open, my foot propping it up.

I came to America to find myself, but this is what I've got—a girl who believes that if everyone thinks she's dead, she'll finally get to live.

It's time to break protocol. I call Kayla's parents.

Deep breaths, and then I get ready to lie. Lie because if I don't, things will be even worse. That's what I tell myself, anyway.

The thoroughly pleasant woman who has been hosting me for the past year answers the phone.

I talk: "Mrs. McPherson? I'm at the beach. Kayla wanted to take the jet ski out early, before it gets crowded. But, something went wrong. She hasn't come back."

I pull the phone back as a flurry of worried expressions explode from the tiny speaker. My pulse pounds so hard I can't listen. I did it: I set Kayla's death loose on the world.

2. The search

FROM BLUE MORNING TO BLACK NIGHT. We caught the edge of the front, storms bursting around us. The wind cuts across the gulf, slings saltwater up from the bay into my face. My clothes and hair are stiff with it, skin raw: I've been at the beach for twenty-one hours.

A whistle blows three times in quick succession, faint over the sound of waves on the shore. In response, the dozen flashlights within a hundred yards of me become alert, unwavering glare focusing on the source of the sound. Satisfied, they return to their task—dozens of them, bobbing in the dark, great hollow eyes hunting the ground for any sign of Kayla.

I push through the gnarled mass of oceanside bush, almost losing my footing in the process. The sand glows faintly in the moonlight, and miles of raw Texas coast stretch out around me. After hours of searching, I am returning to the pier where the police set up a checkpoint. It's two in the morning, and the whistle means we're supposed to quit.

I stop at a knotted log, half devoured by sand. No way around—I can only climb, or swim.

Too tired to do either; I take a moment to shine my light on the glistening bay. The surface is black gloss, a dark skin pulsating. Port Lavaca's causeway stretches across the water, lit by dim yellow street lights in perfect intervals. A single black car rolls across, soundless in the night.

"Let me give you a hand."

I turn to see one of our friends from school, who turned out in droves as word spread. A foot long black flashlight is clenched under his arm, and he's got one leg on the log. He pulls himself up, then offers a hand to me. We grip each other's wrists and use the tension in our arms to balance as we cross the waist-high obstruction.

"Kayla!" he yells out as we reach the other side, the next pocket of beach. The only response is a rising chorus of similar calls, as other searchers are reminded to keep crying out to her.

"I hope she's okay," I murmur.

"We all do," he says, patting me on the back.

Our two lights meet a third, a girl who graduated with Kayla—I can't remember her name. We walk wordlessly to a fourth light, and our constellation grows.

A loathsome wail tears across the beach, the sound of a woman shrieking the lost girl's name. We can't see her, but we know the source: Kayla's mother.

As we trudge back, our numbers grow. Mostly Kayla's or my friends from school, and a few police officers and firemen. People rub my shoulder, turn to me and offer broken smiles of encouragement. The assumption is that I'm taking it especially hard, because I saw her last, and because for the past year I've lived under the same roof as Kayla.

The parking lot is in view, and four police cars at ninety degree angles to each other form a makeshift base camp for the operation.

I could tell them all the truth. But what's the truth? For all I know, Kayla may really be washed up on the shore somewhere. She still hasn't called.

We cross to the pavement of the parking lot; one of the police car's headlights flare to life, blinding me. The group stops, shields their eyes.

"Sean Reilly?" someone calls from beyond the light.

"Yeah?" I call back into the glow.

The lights dim. Purple blotches invade my vision as I squint at a broad-shouldered police officer with a clipboard in his hands.

"You're Sean Reilly?" he asks.

I walk up to him; he's an inch shorter, but probably twice my weight. An LED light is clipped to the brim of his black cap, and shines down at the sheet on his board. When he looks up, pale blue light beams into my eyes.

"You are the last person who saw Kayla McPherson?" he asks, jaw square, eyes sunken. There is this exhausted rigidity to him, a tension that holds him in place, but only barely.

I nod.

"Describe the last time you saw her, please," he says.

The first thing I say to someone is always a throwaway, at least in this country. I start the sentence slow, on purpose. "Right here, in the bay, riding her jet ski," I say.

His eyes widen. "Where are you from? Wait, let me guess."

"Cork," I say, before he does. I hate it when they guess. "I'm from a city called Cork, in the Republic of Ireland. I'm an exchange student."

"Good to meet you, Sean from Cork. I'm Dan, from the police department." He extends a hand, and I reach out to take it. We shake once; he squeezes too hard, like a threat and a greeting all at once. Texans.

"Why did you two come out here so early?" he asks.

I turn back; more searchers stream in, crestfallen, lights hanging limp as they cross into the parking lot.

"She came and woke me up early, shook me out of bed. Told me she wanted to take the jet ski out and ride while the sun rose." I wipe sweat off my forehead with a heavy hand. "She needed my help to get it hitched and unhitched, and to back the trailer into the water. Kayla's always terrified she's going to sink her truck."

He glances up from his writing. "Go on," he prods. "What time did you get out here?"

"About five thirty," I say. "I haven't gone home since."

"And then what?" he asks.

"I helped her get it into the water. I didn't want to go out; I wore this," I point down at my shorts and sandals. "Too cold, in the morning. I just went for her, you know? It all happened right there." I point to the pier. Her truck is still parked in the same place.

"When she went out, was she wearing a life jacket?"

"No," I lie.

He writes this down on his pad. Then he leans in and squints at me, lowers his voice and speaks softly. "And did you check how much gas was in the jet ski before she left?"

"No," I lie. "Did you find the jet ski?"

He points to the water. A boat arrives, pulling parallel to the small wooden pier. Trailing behind is a swell of water; something is being dragged along, barely breaking the surface.

The boat stops, and two men on the pier throw hooks into the bay, as another man wades down the nearby boat ramp. A truck trails him, and soon, a winch tows Kayla's jet ski up the ramp. The little craft is almost completely submerged, and as it's lifted from the bay, water pours out.

"It sank?" I ask. I didn't even know they could sink.

"Apparently," the policeman answers. "Don't know why it sank. They found it a mile out, bobbing half underwater."

"Oh," I say quietly.

He drops the clipboard, lets it rest at his waist. There's another long moment where I'm still and he's staring at me. "What the hell happened?" he asks.

"I don't know. I want to help—I want her to be okay." My voice cracks as I say the words. It does this because what I'm saying is true.

His eyes soften. "We all want to find Kayla, son," he says. "Keep praying."

That's not completely true, though. Kayla, in particular, does not want to be found. If you asked her, she'd tell you she finally succeeded in murdering her shadow.

3. Conscience

THE SILENCE IN THE HOME of Kayla McPherson is not the absence of sound, but an entity unto its own. It is thick and you breathe it. The stifling byproduct of helpless rage, an anger which consumes itself and leaves this haunted hush in its wake.

No one even asked if I'd be going to school today, so I'm not.

By noon, a need for coffee drives me out of my bedroom. On the way to the kitchen, I pass Mr. McPherson. He sits on the recliner, gripping the sides of the chair, staring into a black television.

There's still some in the carafe, so I pour it into a mug and place this in the microwave.

"There's no cream." His hollow voice comes unbidden from the living room.

"That's okay," I call.

I start to say something else, to use this as a gateway to some warming conversation. The thought flickers and dies; that horrible silence burns the oxygen from the room.

On the way back to my room, I pass Kayla's. The walls are bare, but not because her parents don't try to put things up. She takes it down, stuffs it under her bed.

I return to my room, shut the door, and find my phone buzzing. It's been this way since yesterday—a text message a minute. Everyone I go to school with is asking what happened, if the police found Kayla, if I'm all right. I answer a few, until it's clear I can't keep up.

There's only one person I want to hear from, anyway, and she hasn't called.

There's a timid knock on my bedroom door. "Sean? You want lunch?"

The voice is dry and thin. The little pleasant inflections are forced, straining the words to their breaking point. Kayla's mom is the last person on Earth I want to deal with.

"Not really," I say through the door. "I had a big breakfast."

She's coming, either way. I toss my mobile phone into the nightstand drawer—Kayla might call that phone. Then I stretch to turn on a lamp, nearly knocking over the little four-leaf-clover alarm clock Kayla's mom gave me when I first got here. Hate that gift shop crap, honestly, but it was sweet of her to think of me.

The door cracks open. A woman in her early fifties with red eyes, sagging cheeks, and oily hair enters. She holds one clutched fist to her mouth, always an inch away from chewing on a nail—nails that are jagged like splintered boards, some gnawed down to the flesh.

Her only child has been missing for thirty-six hours.

Mrs. McPherson takes a few steps forward, fully entering my room, and stands there with one hand on the round, wooden bedpost near my feet. She stares at me, neither of us speaking, her grief a sickly heat. I'm not exactly pleased with the situation myself, and I think she feels my dismay as well. Feedback loop of despair.

"It's not your fault," she says. "You're a good, responsible kid. I know that. It's Kayla's jet ski, she knows to check the plugs and gas. I don't want you to blame yourself."

Stab me in the heart. "Thank you," I whisper. "What do you mean, check the plugs?"

"Oh, I talked to the police. The drain plugs were out, that's why it sank."

I want to ask her what a drain plug is, but her eyes are wet, and I don't push.

Death eats away at Mrs. McPherson—the death I unleashed on Kayla's behalf. She spread it to the people she should want to protect most.

Stupid, selfish girl.

Just call me, you stupid, selfish girl.

Mrs. McPherson takes another step forward, and I see she wants to hug, so I lean up in the bed to make it easier. Her arms reach past, wrap around me; she smells like weak deodorant and strong sweat. My arms are around her, and her head passes mine, sharp chin pressing into my shoulder.

So frail. A little whimper escapes her, and I feel her body quiver. Hummingbird brittle, shivering wreck of a creature.

I can see the nightstand out the corner of my eye. Can't help but think about the cell phone—her daughter could call it any minute. If she did, right now, I swear I'd let Mrs. McPherson answer. Let her know that Kayla is alive.

If she is. Just call, damnit.

4. Conspirators

IF THERE IS ONE PERSON WHO KNOWS MORE THAN ME about the fate of Kayla McPherson, it's Jack. She talks about him, and I've driven her to his house a few times. The house I'm standing behind now.

Her boyfriend, maybe. One thing I'm sure of, is that he's the man who taught her how to die—so, there is nowhere else for me to be. Not at school, not in therapy, and not asleep.

My fist hits the screen door and the door rebounds against the frame, plastic and aluminum flexing. I repeat this in a series of snare drum pops, in groups of five.

I step back to observe. I'm shaded by a lone oak tree, but the sun beams into my eyes when it shoots between shifting leaves. His yard is more acorn than grass, like most of them in this neighborhood. A poor part of town, every home identical, single story and made from wood. Everywhere I look, I see cars on blocks and kid's bikes laying in the lawn next to plastic ornaments.

Just before I start knocking again, I hear motion from within the house, and freeze.

A woman appears through the translucent panel of the screen door. Dark brown hair straight, down below her shoulders. Broad forehead freckle-specked. The faintest wrinkles around her eyes and lips suggest she might be mid-twenties, early thirties. Face clean, barely any makeup.

"I'm Morgan," she says, smiling. "Who are you?"

"Sorry—I'm looking for Jack, it's urgent." Then I realize she's asked a question. "I'm Sean," I stammer.

"Nice accent," she comments. "You're trying to not sell anything, are you?"

"I just need to talk to Jack. He lives here, doesn't he?"

"I'm sorry, but I don't know anyone named Jack."

Didn't expect this. I step back, look around the back yard. This is definitely the house I remember.

"I know he's been here before. He stood right there: skinny, pale, bald head."

She becomes rigid, and something quiet takes control of her face. The smile fades, replaced by a subtle, fixed calm. Smooth, like a stone from the river.

"I need to talk about Kayla McPherson."

This gets a response: the edges of her eyes and cheeks crack alive.

"Come in," she says.

I enter. Low light streams in from thin curtains over brown-specked windows. The kitchen is dirty: dishes in the sink, trash piled high above the trash can.

I hesitate at the threshold to the living room. There is no furniture. Instead, there's a large flat screen television, guarded by two waist-high speakers. A pile of movies spreads out against one wall, like a black rot. Bands of black film jut out below silver discs, torn loose from ancient VHS tapes.

Each of the titles is in French, and appears to be black and white; probably old, from the forties or fifties.

"Brilliant," I mumble. "You watch all of these?"

She nods, smiling. "La Nouvelle Vague." The French rolls off her tongue. "Trying to see every New Wave film. You know: Truffaut, Godard, Rohmer, Charbroil, and everyone inspired by them. You need to have projects."

I don't know. Couldn't tell if those are names, or places, or titles of films, so I remain silent.

Morgan doesn't seem to mind the mess; she walks across some of the little silver plates on the floor. I follow her into a narrow hall. Everything is bare, not a single picture hanging. Like they just moved in, and don't own anything but a massive television and a collection of French movies.

There's an open door to the right. Plastic wrap spreads into the hallway; when I turn, I see the sheet covers the room. It's dim, as the only light streams through tattered curtains.

Jack leans over a tragic humanoid figure; a half-formed clay statue, still wet. He's crafting a mud homunculus in the form of a woman's upper body, arms outstretched from the floor. Her damp, crude upper half seems to break out of the carpet, hands clawing out for a grip to pull her still sunken legs free.

He's wearing headphones, nodding to a beat, and shaping her. A pile of clay sits nearby, and a bucket of water next to that. His hands are caked in white. Head shaved, skeletal thin, with a tattoo on the inside of his bony forearm reading "freedom from myself."

I bang on the frame of the door with my closed fist. Jack jolts as he looks up; he jerks in surprise, and the entire right arm of the sculpture comes away in his grip.

Jack glares at the severed clay limb in frustration, then hurls it on the plastic below. It lands with a wet splat, base spreading across the sheet so that her arm appears to sink back into whatever netherworld she struggled out of.

"Shit," he exclaims, red-faced, looking at the ruined figure, then at Morgan and I. "You gotta come and surprise me like that? You think that's funny?"

I say nothing, only stare at him. He stares back.

Morgan clears her throat.

My voice is low. "You probably don't remember me. I picked Kayla up, dropped her off a few times."

"Yeah? You want some pot, or what?" he asks, arms dropping to his sides, chalk-white from sculpting. "You're at the wrong house. I don't do ten dollar drug deals with teenagers."

"I lived with her family for the past year. I know what she planned, why she disappeared. I know about her shadow."

Jack takes a step closer to me, and the plastic crinkles noisily underfoot. "What do you think you know about shadows?"

"I found a duffel bag full of money in her room. She told me what she planned, you know, with her death. Kayla said she would call me when she crossed the gulf. She didn't, though. I need to know if she's okay."

Jack pulls an electronic cigarette from his pocket and puts it to his lips. The tip glows blue when he inhales, and an odorless white cloud streams from his nostrils. "Maybe she just doesn't want to talk to you," he says.

"I don't—" I stop mid-sentence. Not sure what to make of that. "She *promised* she would call me. That was our plan."

"Normal people can't understand. Kayla liberated herself; she doesn't want anything to do with you anymore. Not with anyone."

"Did you talk to her?" I ask. "You know she's okay?"

He points out the window, e-cig perched between two fingers. "When you get out there, when you clear everything, something changes. You don't want to be bothered. You only want to engage. Kayla is realizing who she is for the first time in her life, and she is happier than she's ever been."

"I asked if you talked to her." I want facts, not more of his bullshit.

Jack waves a hand, swatting my question out of the air. "What's the difference, really? I mean, you're never going to see her again, no matter what. She's dead to you either way. Right?"

My fingers are so tight around the door frame, it takes a conscious effort on my part to release them. He makes me nervous.

"That's not the point," I say, then pause, flustered. "Stop talking like that, be straight with me. I haven't told anyone anything, because she begged me not to. But, I don't know what the hell a drain plug is, or why the jet ski sank. It was supposed to run out of gas, and she would swim to shore. I need to tell the police. That wasn't an accident—someone made it sink."

Morgan speaks quickly: "The police are already searching everywhere. If something happened to Kayla, we've already done everything we can do. They'll find her. Telling the police about her plan just gets everyone in trouble, including her, if Jack is right and she's safe. It's of no use to anyone. Right?"

"I don't mean to be rude, but who are you, anyway?" I ask her.

"I told you," she says, face smiling but eyes not. "I'm Morgan."

"I want to know if anyone has talked to Kayla," I repeat. "Either of you. I can't just abandon her if she's hurt. I need to know what happened."

Jack walks over to me and puts a hand on the door frame, inches from my face—though upon noticing he's left a clay handprint, he pulls away. As he inhales again on the electronic cigarette, it makes a soft crackling sound. All the while, his eyes never leave mine.

I don't back away—just tense up, in case he tries to hit me, which seems likely.

Before he can act, though, Morgan speaks again: "She had a car waiting, on the coast, for when she got to the other side. We can go check the spot. If the car's gone, you know she made it. If it's still there, well, we've got a problem."

"How do you know all this?"

She ignores my question. "The car is pretty well out of sight, so I'll have to go with you. You driving?"

5. Causeway

A ONE-MILE CAUSEWAY stretches across the shipping channel in Port Lavaca's corner of the bay; the same massive bridge I watched from the beach that long night of searching for Kayla's body. The center of the bridge arches upward, rising yards above the rest, allowing ships to pass underneath. We cross that now, gulf dropping away below us.

"Are you from around here?" I ask, spinning the old manual crank to lower my window.

"I'm not really from around anywhere," Morgan says, pulling rogue strands of brown hair behind her ear as wind rushes through. "What about you? You from around here?"

I smile at her joke. She smiles back. Nice smile, rows of straight teeth. Face and arms dusted with freckles; reminds me of home. Even if she is a little old for me.

"Shame about the view," I say, nodding at the coastline ahead of us.

"It's like the beach has cancer."

And she's right, Port Lavaca is infected. A growth of metal pipes, smokestacks, compressed gas. Pressurized chambers of toxic gas; burners and steel drums. It's an industrial town, and the only reason people live here are the five refineries. They emerge malignant from the pale, peach coast. Tanks tower hundreds of feet in the air, connected with labyrinthine pipes. The knotted steel is crowned with flare stacks burning ten-foot red flames.

There is no view of the coast that isn't spoiled by this metallic mutation, this metastasis of steel and plastic.

I'm told that from time to time, the refineries explode, as well. So many great things about them, really.

"Turn here," she says as we reach the other end of the bridge. I hesitate as I make the left turn, starting then stopping again. She glances at me.

"You all drive on the wrong side of the road," I comment.

"Is this her truck?" Morgan asks.

"Yeah." And then I notice her favorite albums, the cellophane from her last pack of cigarettes, a hair brush with a rubber grip. Like being in Kayla's mind.

I shrink away from it all. She could be dead.

We near a refinery where bauxite is turned to aluminum. The entire area is coated in ruddy dust, so it seems every car and building has been meticulously painted reddish brown. Looks like Mars.

"Turn right, before the gate," she says.

I stop short of the secure, gated entrance to the plant and turn right on a dirt road. I follow this into a cove, sheltered by a wall of mesquite trees.

"Turn here."

Off this road, another, and finally a narrow path whose presence is only betrayed by the two parallel lines of trampled shrubbery.

I drive down the path; the waves lap at the shell-clad beach a few yards off. Straight across the bay sits the dock where I last saw Kayla.

"Get as close as you can. The car was behind these trees."

When I reach a thicket, I stop the truck and get out. I walk past the line of gnarled trees and bramble bushes. Baited breath.

Please don't be here. Please don't let there be a car sitting here, untouched.

I step into the clearing.

Nothing, just sand and weeds.

"All right, then." I smile. "So she made it this far. She made it to her car." A lot easier to accept she may just not want to call me, that Jack is right.

We get back in the truck, and head back the direction we came. Feeling like there may be hope for her after all. If she climbed out of the gulf, landed here and drove away—she must be safe, right? The gulf is the dangerous part, the swimming. This, plus the fact the police haven't found a body, let me think she might be okay.

The causeway passes under us again, rhythmic bumps of the expansion joints bucking the truck like a train over tracks.

"So, how did you get involved in all this?" I ask Morgan.

She's silent.

We cross back into Port Lavaca; the sun is setting behind us and casts a neon dusk, a fifteen minute span where the blues, oranges and pinks of the sky seem radioactive.

I try again to engage her. "So what's this 'shadow' stuff Jack was going on about? Kayla talked the same crap. What are they talking about?"

My comment doesn't seem to register on Morgan's face. "Jack does love to talk crap," she murmurs.

The car falls to silence again. Then, moments later:

"Sean, are you speeding?" she asks.

I look down at my speedometer. I'm not; I try not to. Never break the law in a foreign country—advice from Dad, before I left.

"There's a policeman following us," she says. "Drive carefully."

I glance in my rear view. Monochrome suburban, rack of lights and black bull bars. "It's probably nothing," I say, though suddenly my body feels tight.

"Listen to me, Sean. Turn right, right here."

"That's not the way back."

"Just turn."

I do. The policeman follows. Now I'm driving slowly into a neighborhood I don't know.

Morgan's voice is tense and low. "Sean, I need you to pay attention to me. I think something has gone wrong. We've been betrayed. I think he's going to turn on his lights. This is very important: You cannot talk about me when you talk about Kayla. You have to keep my name out of it."

"What are you talking about?"

Blue and red lights fill my rear windshield; kaleidoscopic calamity.

"I can help you, but you must trust me. Tell them you picked me up across the bridge, that I'm a hitchhiker. I'm not real, Sean. I'm not a real person."

"How can a person not be real?"

She doesn't answer.

I put the truck in park, turn on the hazard lights. There's a cop standing in front of my open window. He speaks: "Are you Sean Reilly?" he asks.

Getting this question a lot, lately. "Yeah," I say. "That's me."

"We want to ask you some questions. You mind coming with me?"

6. Detective

As a boy, I had trouble sleeping. My dad taught me how to count my breath: each exhale is a number. Up to ten, then you start over again. You'd be surprised how hard it is to count ten breaths without getting distracted. The point is to keep your mind focused, so you don't worry and wander. Most of the time, people worry themselves into worse trouble than what they were worried about in the first place.

That's what Dad says, anyway. I'm doing a lot of counting, now. Harder than I ever counted before.

Not under arrest, at least I don't think. But I am deep in the police station, in a private little room with two chairs, a table, and a camera mounted on the ceiling. I watched them put Morgan in the room next door.

I breathe out. One.

The door to the interrogation room opens.

"Sean Reilly," a man says as he enters. "I'm Detective Alvarado. I'm investigating the disappearance of Kayla McPherson."

He's about my height, six foot. Face pitted with decades old acne scars, black hair dusted with gray. Mexican, broad shoulders. He's old, mid-fifties, and his mouth tilts downward in disapproval, although I haven't said anything yet.

Two.

"You're from Ireland, aren't you?"

I nod.

Three.

He pulls a silver pair of spectacles from his shirt pocket and places them on his nose. "How long are you here for?"

"Maybe a few years, until after college. Maybe forever, if I find a job here," I say. My voice is very quiet; quieter than I mean it to be.

Four.

"And you're a senior? So you're graduating, then. Okay. And you stay in the same house as Kayla, correct?" As he speaks, he is preoccupied with the portfolio in his lap, arranging the pages within. He only glances up on the last word of each sentence.

"Yes," I say.

Five.

"Must be strange, for an eighteen year old boy to find himself under the same roof as a nineteen year old girl, someone he isn't related to, you know? Hormones, and all that?"

"There is some of that," I admit.

Six.

"Seeing each other half-dressed, spending all that alone time together. Is that exciting?"

I shrug, but can feel my cheeks turning red.

Now, all his attention is on me. His hands rest on the table, across the halfway mark courtesy would designate as my half. "Did you like her?" he asks, leaning in.

"She's very dramatic. Very serious. She'll be pissed at you for a week, and you won't ever find out why." Then I admit it: "But yeah, I liked her a little bit."

Seven.

"How much is a little bit?" he asks.

"Well, I probably spent more time with Kayla than anyone else here in the States, you know?"

"Did she like you back?" he asks, folding his hands on the white plastic table between us. A gold wedding band, silver watch. It bothers me that they don't match.

"Not like that," I say. "But, it's okay. I'm probably not going to be in this town after I graduate, so I didn't plan on meeting any girls."

Eight.

"Did you kill her because she didn't like you back?" He asks this like everything else, like it's a normal question.

I lose count.

"Is she dead?" I ask.

Every time I lose count, I have to start over.

Detective Alvarado leans back, grips the sides of his navy blazer and pulls it tight around his shoulders. Then he watches me, saying nothing. I think he's waiting for me to confess, to spill my guts. I count all the way to ten again before he asks another question.

"Port Lavaca is a small place," he says. "I know almost everyone who knows Kayla; I know their parents. I know who is trouble, and who isn't. What I don't know is you, or the girl we found you with. Who is she?"

One.

"I just picked her up," I say. "She was walking across the causeway, looked like she needed a lift."

The detective smirks. "Is that right? Just met her? What a coincidence. Tell me the truth, Sean."

Two.

"I did. Is Kayla dead? I need to know."

The detective leans back, says nothing.

I continue: "Is that why I'm in here, all of a sudden? Did you find her?"

Three.

He speaks: "My goal here is to be completely transparent with you. I'm going to tell you everything that's on my mind, and you can be honest with me, or you can dig your hole deeper. I'm going to find the truth, either way. You said you got to the beach around five thirty in the morning. You also said that you didn't get in the water, only Kayla did. You called her parents around nine. Why did it take you over three hours to call someone?"

Shit. Lost count again.

"I was scared," I say. "I figured Kayla would come back. What if she was playing a joke? I didn't want the police looking for her over a joke."

He pulls a photograph from the file in his lap. It's a picture of a neon blue life jacket—the life jacket Kayla wore, the one I lied about.

"We found this on the coast. See the writing on the back? That's from the Emerald Point Marina up in Austin. Pretty unique. Kayla's parents confirm they own one exactly like it, except theirs is missing. You said Kayla wasn't wearing a life jacket. I say the odds that's not their life jacket are a million to one. Wouldn't you? Now, how did it get from Kayla's home to being washed up on the beach?"

Damnit. No counting, now. How did that happen? What happened to Kayla?

"I took it," I say quickly.

"I believe that, but not for the reasons you may think. You said you weren't going in the water," he reminds me.

Christ. Panicking, now, so I don't say anything. He watches me. Can feel him summing me up.

I smooth my hair twice in a row, too fast, too jittery. The detective cracks a grin. It's obvious I'm freaked.

He withdraws another photograph. I see it, but don't.

It's antimatter; I see it, and it sees me, and we cancel each other out. Mind won't register. Can't. A tiny whimper betrays me, squeezes through the tension I ratcheted myself up with.

The detective speaks: "You said Kayla got on the jet ski alone, but that was you. You killed Kayla the night before, and spent all morning staging this crime scene. After you tried to sink her body, you went home, took the drain plugs out of the jet ski and brought it to the beach. After it sank, you swam back to shore with the life jacket on. Then you told your story. If we never found her body, we'd assume she drowned. You cut her throat."

The picture on the table is Kayla. Her face stares up at me, blue veins clawing up pale, bloated flesh. A deep gash stretches across her throat.

7. Truth

HOLY SHIT. This can't be happening—Kayla can't be dead. I lean back and put both hands to my forehead. The world spins, so I close my eyes. I take ten deep breaths, trying to hold back the tears and the panic.

It doesn't work. In this instant, my world is gone.

I open my eyes to a fresh oblivion. Detective Alvarado leans back and watches me. The picture stays on the table, staring skyward with milky eyes. "Now, tell me what happened," he says.

I decide that I will. Somewhere, something has gone terribly wrong. Don't need to keep my promise to a dead girl.

"Kayla tried to fake her own death. She got the idea from someone she knows, a guy named Jack."

"Jack who?" he asks.

"Jack Vickery."

"Why would Kayla want to fake her death?"

"Lots of reasons. For one thing, the money. Jack has these fake ID's, he says he's made millions on life insurance policies, just scamming the system. Pretending he's dead, then cashing in a policy on himself and starting over as someone new."

The detective's eyes narrow. "That sounds like horse shit. Is that the best you've got? Why would a nineteen year old girl with parents who provide for her want to go through all that trouble?"

I start to talk about shadows, but then decide not to. I sound crazy enough already. "Kayla made it sound very romantic. She asked me—who is a person, really? If you destroy your identity, if you cut all ties and fake your death, then what's left? Something without labels, something with money and freedom. Plus—" I stop. This part is harder to say.

"Yeah?" He's clearly not buying this.

"She wanted everyone to miss her. She wanted to see her own funeral."

"This is the stupidest—someone cut her throat, then tried to sink the body. And right now, if someone asked me who did it, I'd point them at you. You want to talk about labels? How about 'felon,' how does that suit you? How about 'death row inmate?'"

My face heats up, molten material in my eyes. Words spill out: "She didn't even want me to know about this. I found a bag of money under her bed, and I asked her about it. When she told me, it sounded made up—I didn't think anything would happen. I figured she'd back out."

"Tell me everything," he says.

"I just did what she said. I drained the gas from the jet ski, so it would barely run. We timed the whole thing for when the tide went out. Kayla would drive it out into the bay, go in a few circles until it died. Then she'd swim to the beach on the opposite side—a long way, but she wore a life jacket, and she could do a back stroke. Apparently she left a car waiting—it's gone now, I checked—so she could disappear with the money. I would call someone to help after she let me know she made it. Except, she didn't call, so I got stuck there. I panicked and called her parents. So, what am I really guilty of? I lied about a life jacket, and waited a while to tell anyone she was missing. I figured she was okay."

"You're lying again. You left out the drain plugs," he says.

"Will someone tell me what a goddamn drain plug is?"

The detective snorts out half a laugh, then reaches into the folder again. He draws out a picture and flips it on the table, dealing my hand.

This time, it's a close-up of the back of the jet ski. There are two black holes, each the size of a silver dollar.

"That's where the drain plugs go. You take those out, then turn the jet ski off in some water? It'll sink in a couple of minutes."

"I had no idea," I tell him. "You have to believe me. I never took apart their jet ski, why would I? It's not mine."

"You're lying."

"I'm not lying! Find Jack Vickery," I say. "He is the only other person who knew Kayla's plan, as far as I know. He can tell you that I'm telling the truth."

"Jack Vickery. What does he look like?"

I start to talk, then stumble over my words. "Bald, skinny, shorter than me. He has a tattoo, on the inside of his left arm—says 'freedom from myself' in old typewriter font. Look, if you put him in front of me, I can point him out."

The detective shakes his head, seems exhausted with disbelief. "I'm going to go talk to your friend," he says. "See if she says anything different. And if she does, guess what? That's one more in a growing list of reasons I want to put you on trial."

It's been an hour since the detective left me to go speak with Morgan. Can't stop thinking about her. What's she saying?

She could make me seem guilty. Just a little bit of suspicion, and it would be that much worse for me. Maybe she'll throw me to the wolves, to save herself.

Morgan did say she could help me. What does that mean?

We barely know each other. She's vulnerable in there, too. All she needs to do is tell a little lie: say I'm in love with Kayla, or say she's seen me act violent before. I'm teetering on the knife's edge, here. A little push and I'll be going to court for sure.

I should have acted first, when I had his ear. Should have told him Morgan is involved, that she lived with Jack. Let her go down with me.

Just want to come clean, be done with this whole mess. I didn't kill anyone. They'll see. They'll use forensics and they'll see I didn't do it.

Detective Alvarado opens the door.

"Sean Reilly, stand up," he says.

I do so.

"You have the right to remain silent; anything you say can be used against you in a court of law. You have the right to an attorney. The Irish Consulate will be notified of your arrest."

He drones on, but I can't hear over the howling distortion in my head. The rush of emotion is deafening: terror, anger and anxiety override me.

Two more officers push into the tiny room. They're huge, twice as much muscle as me. Someone grabs my arms, and handcuffs tighten around my wrists.

"We asked the McPherson's permission to search your room. Guess what we found in your closet?" Something hard drops on the table, landing with a knock. In a clear, plastic evidence bag sit two black plugs, ringed stems protruding from both. They look like tiny hand grenades. "'What's a drain plug,' right?"

8. Cell

"DINNER TIME," a guard says, unlocking the cell where I'm caged. Once the bolt is released, he walks past.

I move hesitantly to the gate, but can't see anything other than the gray brick wall in front of me. With the bars in hand, I pull; they slide back, opening. I step outside, into the stone and cement passage.

A line of men in orange uniforms march toward me, heading from their cells down the hallway.

"Hey!" one of them shouts. "White boy!"

I freeze, not sure what to do. Act tough? Be friendly? The only thing I know about jail comes from television.

The four men approach; I press against the wall so they can pass. Each are Hispanic, necks marked with tattoos.

When the second man passes, he pivots suddenly, and pain wracks my skull; I'm blinded by flashing lights. He's thrown a haymaker, punched me in the side of the head.

I slide down to the ground as the world recombobulates, pieces of sight returning at a time—first simple contrast, then shapes and colors. The men laugh as they continue past, shouting something at me in Spanish before disappearing down the hall.

Shit. My whole skull hurts; I climb to my feet, scared someone else will find me and attack. I pull my cell back open, walk inside, and close the door.

It's becoming abundantly clear to me that a skinny eighteen year old foreigner will not be welcome in a South Texas jail. If I even make it to a court date, it'll be luck getting me there.

Trap a rabbit in a cage, and he wants out. Put that cage in a lion's den, and he wants to stay in.

I do not sleep so much as keep watch. Sometime in the night—late enough that it may be morning—I hear footsteps. A man appears in front of my cell. His hands are stuffed in the pockets of a tan windbreaker, which he clutches to his body like a bat wraps itself in its wings. His gut is outlined by the synthetic fabric, and shielded partly by a faded gold plate of a belt buckle.

"Are you Sean Reilly?" he asks in a whisper.

Curled brown hair peels back from his scalp. Coffee eyes squint at me, wrinkles twisting in on themselves.

"Yeah?" I ask. "That's me."

"My name is Sheriff Cole Durham. I'm from Sonoma County, California. We can't talk long, so listen careful. I believe Jack Vickery is real, and the police here don't."

I study him. His forehead shines in the yellow light, the result of a reflective sheen of sweat that he rubs back from his eyes with the back of his hand. He smells stale, breath and body odor a foul alchemy.

"Well, go talk to the detective! No one else believes me."

"They don't believe me either, not anymore. I've chased the son of a bitch for three years. He killed my wife, same way he killed Kayla. Convinced her to fake her death, then took her out. Listen, I'm going to give you a piece of paper with my number, put it in your sock. Call me when you get out."

He glances down the hall, eyes sweeping the corridor. Cole sniffs, then scratches at his nose. "They're about to send the consul in here to talk with you. Listen, this is real important: When you met Jack, was there a woman with him?"

Morgan?

I hesitate, words shaken by my tremoring jaw, still sore from getting punched.

The sound of a door opening. Cole glances to his left, then faces me. "Take this, I have to go. Now, take it."

I take the scrap of paper from his hand and slip it into my pocket.

"Call me," he says, then turns and steps out of view.

Moments later, a prison guard and a man in a suit appear in front of my cell. The man in the suit seems to be shrinking away from the walls, clutching a blazer to his shoulders.

"Sean Reilly?" he asks. His voice brings a wave of relief: an Irish accent.

"Yeah?"

"I'm Patrick Dore; I'm from the Irish Consulate in Houston. How are you?" His voice dips when he asks that—he knows the answer pretty well.

"Horrible," I hiss. "Get me out of here."

"Were you attacked?" he asks, pointing at the side of his face.

"Someone punched me in the hall, for no reason. I can't even go out there to eat. They're going to kill me in here."

The consul stares at his shoes for a moment, salt and pepper stubble rising from his sunken jaw. "The judge posted bail," he says. "If you can pay it, you can stay out of jail until the trial. But—the bail is set at five hundred thousand, and you'll need to give up your passport and driver's permit."

Feels like a punch to my stomach. "Five hundred...?"

"You only need to pay fifty thousand of that to a bondsman, and they'll let you out. As long as you show up for court, you'll get the money back."

Like that's much better. "Only fifty thousand?" I ask, dripping sarcasm.

"Would be twice as much if you weren't so young," he says. "Do you have any money?"

"My parents might," I say, "Do they know what's happened?"

"My people are trying to reach them now," he assures me.

I grab hold of one of the steel bars, feel its pitted surface as I drag my hand down. "Why am I in here?" I ask. "I'm innocent."

"I heard the police's story. They think you killed Kayla late that night—"

"—I was in bed!"

"I don't believe them either, Sean, I'm only telling you what I know. Listen, they think you killed Kayla late that night, drove home, got the jet ski, and sank it to fake the whole scene."

"That's ridiculous!" I'm almost shouting.

Someone down the hall yells an obscenity, tells us to shut up.

"Sean, you lied to the police three times. About the gasoline and the life jacket—which you admitted to—and about the drain plugs."

"Someone put those drain plugs in my closet. I'm being set up—find Jack Vickery, he knows everything."

He glances down. "They looked into that, Sean. They can't find any sign someone named Jack Vickery lived in Port Lavaca."

Useless. It's beginning to dawn on me that maybe Jack did more than teach Kayla how to fake her death—maybe he killed her, and framed me. Who else could it be?

"Where's my lawyer?" I ask. "Don't I get a lawyer? Someone to help me?"

He puts a hand to the crimson tie at his throat and adjusts it. "The public defender is reviewing your case now. I can connect you to a friendlier attorney, someone with ties to the consulate. You'll need to pay for it, though."

"More money—great. So, what can you actually do for me?"

The consul presents his hands, palms upward. "Do you want me to pray with you?"

I turn away, curse under my breath. "So, nothing. Just let my parents know what's happened, okay? Make sure they know."

He nods, puts his hands in his pockets. "Keep your faith, Sean. Things will work out."

Things won't work out. I'll get the death penalty. They'll strap me to a table, inject me with poison, and I'll die alone in the world except for my executioner and his empty syringe.

I sit on the cot and stare at the hallway for hours, until I hear the movement of guards and smell disinfectant as cleaning begins.

It's not long before the consul returns. He's smiling, blue eyes beaming.

"Your bail was paid," he says. Still happy to hear an Irish accent, even if he's proved himself useless.

I stand. "What? How?" Maybe my parents came through—sold their house, or something.

The consul flips through the papers in his hand, searching for a name. "Sarah Fiesel?" he asks.

"I don't know who that is," I say. "And I don't care. So, I can get out of here?"

"You can," he says. "At least, until the trial."

"How long is that?" I ask as the jail door slides open.

"A few months," he says. "The McPhersons refused to take you; I'm trying to work out a place you can stay."

A pang of guilt strikes just below my Adam's apple. Of course—Kayla's parents think I'm guilty. And they were so nice.

"Mrs. Fiesel offered to rent an extended-stay motel room for you. Is that okay? Is she a relative?"

"It's fine," I say. "She's probably a friend of my parents."

I'm lead through the jail, given my wallet and cell phone back, and shoved out the back door. Rabbit, run.

My phone says I have ninety-nine new text messages, but I think the counter just doesn't go any higher. A dozen missed calls, a handful of voice messages.

Does everyone know I'm the suspect? I don't even look through the texts, just put my phone in my pocket.

The consul leads me to the front of the building. One of Port Lavaca's few taxis is waiting.

He stops at the jailhouse steps. "This taxi will take you to your motel. Whatever you do, do not go near Kayla's home—that's a condition of your bail. Don't do anything stupid, and don't make anything worse on yourself. American police take themselves very seriously," he says. "I'll be in touch. Slán and God bless."

9. Stash

"**R**OUGH DAY?" the taxi driver asks. I watch through the rearview mirror as his brown eyes squint into the sun. I don't even answer. Don't want to do the whole thing; don't want to explain I'm from Cork, or fake-laugh about how funny it is that a city shares a name with a kind of wood. I damn sure don't want to talk about being the suspect in a murder case.

We pull in front of a dingy motel. *The Beach*. Beige paint faded on the side facing the sea, where the salted wind blows hard every day. The sign out front advertises a mini-fridge and free HBO. Home, sweet home.

"I'm totally broke, and I just got out of jail," I tell the cabby when we stop.

"I've been paid," he says. All hostile, now, I guess because I wouldn't talk with him. I open the door and step out.

Two rows of red motel doors face me, with a small office on the far side. I start walking toward the office, but one of the doors opens. A thin, pale arm emerges; I can only just see it from fifty feet away. It beckons for me.

I point at myself, mouthing *me?*

The hand beckons harder. A little nervous tremor starts in my stomach, some fluttering spasm, but I walk over to the door. It's so hot that the tar is sticky, and rocks cling to my trainers when my feet lift from the pitch.

Room 13. The door swings open.

Morgan is inside.

"You?" I ask.

She smiles, freckles shifting across her face, lights across a dance floor. "Me," she says. "Get in here; I can't be seen."

I step inside. Little room, hard gray carpet, smells like cigarettes and piss. "You bailed me out," I say even as I realize it, because it must be true. She's standing here, after all.

"Sarah Fiesel," Morgan says. "For that transaction. If anyone asks, I'm a nurse who worked at Mercy University for your father, and he gave me the money to bail you out."

"How did you..."

"I can search the Internet, Sean. Are you okay?"

I shake my head. I am not ready to be asked that question. "No, not really. Not even close."

Don't know if I've ever felt worse, actually. I'm starving, exhausted. I rub my face and my fingers tremble. "I can't go back."

Morgan steps forward, wraps an arm around my back. I resist, leaning away, but she moves in closer. It's a strange invasion—I barely know her.

But, it feels good. Warm, when I petrified myself so I can survive. When I'm so tired of quivering fear that my whole being is frozen, feeling nothing because if I don't, I'll feel everything.

Then both arms are around me, reaching above my elbows, her hair pressed against my collar. The hard knot in my chest that should be my soul starts to melt. Slowly, my hands come up, hug back.

I realize what's happened, where I am. Arrested for killing Kayla. The lies I told the police, the drain plugs in my closet—the fact I'm the last person to see her alive. It's not over; I'm going back. Back to jail, then to an even worse place, and eventually, strapped to a table and injected with toxins while people watch, happy I'll be dead.

When I open my eyes, I see tears have run down my cheeks and onto the back of Morgan's shirt. Little streaks of wetness, like someone's pricked her with needles. She pats my back, then releases me. I sniff, looking away so she can't see my eyes.

"Get off me," I whisper, scared to talk any louder, because my voice will be cut with a sob. I turn and stare into the clouded mirror which rests over the chipped pewter sink. "I just want to go home. Back to Ireland. I'm done with this country. I miss my parents, my family."

The face in the mirror wastes away. Even paler than usual, brown curls frayed and wild around my head. Eyes sunken, red tinged.

"You didn't tell the police about me," she says. "I appreciate that."

"I told them about Jack, and about Kayla. I told them about everything except you, I had to. I thought it would help," I say. "Just made everything worse. I admitted to lying about the gas, about the life jacket. I admitted to the police that I lied about a missing girl who turned up dead. Oh yeah, and I'm the last person who saw her alive, and I admitted that, too."

"It's okay, Sean."

I run the faucet; it sputters, then spills forth. Little flecks of shaved beard from the last occupant get caught up in the stream, circle the drain and are pulled through.

"What do you want from me?" I ask, voice echoing off the empty sink. "Where's Jack? I think he did this, he set me up. Listen, a man came to my cell last night, seemed real nervous. Said he's a sheriff in California, and that Jack killed his wife the same way Jack killed Kayla."

"The world is full of crazy people."

"It can't be coincidence. Where is Jack?"

"Jack is gone," she answers. "I got you out of prison, and I believe you are being framed. I'm trying to help."

"Yeah, but why? If you really want to help me, then find Jack. He probably murdered her, and if we can get him, maybe the police can prove he did it. At any rate, they'll know I'm not making the whole thing up."

I didn't notice any makeup before, but I see now she's wearing a very subtle lipstick. She speaks: "Jack is out of the picture for the time being. I'm here to help you, and I suggest you go along with it. The alternative is probably the death penalty."

I turn and take a step closer, my eyes averting hers, focusing on her hands instead. The same trick with her lips is at work here. Her fingernails are pale pink, with white tips painted on—like natural fingernails, only better.

"Why should I trust you? I mean, really. I don't know who you are. I don't even know your real name."

She straightens. Something changes in her demeanor; the wet eyes freeze, the smile flattens.

"Sean, it doesn't matter if you trust me. Acting as though you trust me makes sense for you right now; it's your best chance at staying free." Then she pauses; the edges of her lips dip into a frown as her eyes widen. "I'm not going to do a lot of explaining, not now." On this sentence alone, her voice drips sincerity. She's just turned it on, like a tap.

I steel myself, then brave eye contact.

"Tell me what you know about Jack," I demand. "Tell me why you stayed in a house with him."

"No," she answers, words launching through the air, colliding with mine, knocking them off course so they clatter uselessly to the floor. The tap is off again, any hint of kindness gone. Morgan turns away, toward the bed. "Are you hungry? We can order a pizza."

Something about the confidence of her reaction tells me that pushing will get me nowhere.

"I'm starving."

I hear the phone lifted off its receiver; it beeps softly as buttons are pushed. "Come here," she says. "Tell him what you want; we'll pay with cash."

The phone is in my hand, pressed to my ear. "Large pepperoni," I say. "Room 13, at The Beach, the little motel. Cash."

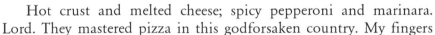

Hot crust and melted cheese; spicy pepperoni and marinara. Lord. They mastered pizza in this godforsaken country. My fingers are slick with grease; it's so hot I can barely hold it, but I can't wait.

She eats one slice. I eat seven.

Morgan brushes off her clothes then stands on the bed, flat green shoes on the comforter. She lifts her arms up to an air vent; as she does this, her shirt lifts, revealing a smooth stomach. The vent's grate comes off in her hands, and we're showered with bits of plaster from the popcorn ceiling.

A duffel bag is crammed into the space. She yanks it down; it flops on the bed. Morgan jumps to the floor, landing softly, and unzips the bag.

Inside: stacks of hundred dollar bills, and a chrome pistol.

"Why are you showing me that?" I ask, nodding at the money and gun.

"In the truck, when I said I could help you, I didn't mean help with your trial," Morgan says, smiling. "I meant I could help you disappear."

"Worked great for Kayla."

"Works well enough for me." Her answer comes quick.

"How much is in there?" I ask as I finish off a crust.

"A lot," she answers. She sits on the bed and crosses her legs.

I walk to the sink, rub my hands on a towel. The rag is thin, absorbs nothing. Still feel greasy. "Why do you have a gun?"

"Don't worry too much about it."

She grips a fat stack of bills, bound with a faded purple band. This is tossed haphazardly on the bed, and the gun follows. Little silver pistol, small enough to be a toy, but heavy enough to sink into the bed sheets.

"Is it like Kayla planned? You got that money faking your death?"

Morgan zips up the bag and shakes it, so the cash settles in the bottom. She runs her hands over the top, and folds the loose part away so that it's a tight rectangular package. All this is done quickly, in practiced motions.

"Yes." She seems reluctant to release the word, escaped from parted lips.

"How does it work?" I ask. "How do you get away with it?"

Half a smile crosses her face. She climbs up on the bed, bag of money in hand, and crams it into the open vent. "Hand me that?" she asks, pointing down at the vent cover.

I pick up the cover, offering it to her. She presses the grate back into place, forcing the screws into the plaster. Once this is done, she folds her legs so they drop out from under her, and flops down to the bed. Morgan bounces on crossed legs like some Yoga master; the bed creaks under her, and the gun bounces too.

"It's not something to talk about," she says.

Still sitting, Morgan picks up the handgun, pulls back the slide and looks through the open chamber, down the barrel.

I sit down in a dingy, floral-patterned chair across the room, out of the way. Can't stop staring. She doesn't point it at me, at least.

"So, earlier in the truck, when you said you're not real, that's because the real you died already—I mean, everyone thinks that?"

The chamber snaps shut. She reaches to the edge of the bed and lifts a large black purse up to her position; the gun and money are placed within.

"That's right," she says.

"So everyone you grew up with thinks you're dead, and you can never let them know you're okay?" I lean back in the chair, crane my neck over the flimsy back and stare at the ceiling. Water damage, like pit stains on a white shirt. "What does that feel like?"

"Freedom."

Morgan walks to her closet, pulls open the particle board cover. A few jackets, jeans, hats, purses. "You're going to be staying in the room next to this one; but first, you need some things, don't you? You didn't bring a bag."

I point at myself. "You're looking at everything I own." I stand, wipe some crumbs from my jeans. Even though I've been up all night, the food gives me energy, feels warm inside. "My stuff is at Kayla's house, but I'm not supposed to go back there."

"We'll buy what you need," she says. Morgan turns and lifts the purse, putting it on her shoulder. The gun is in the purse.

"You've shown me a lot," I say, gesturing vaguely at the ceiling where her money is stashed. "What if I just leave, now? Would you kill me, or what?"

Morgan bites her bottom lip as the corners of her mouth curve upward. "Do you want to die?"

"Do you mean literally die, or figuratively, like you?"

She says nothing, only walks to the door and opens it. I step through.

10. Banks

"**M**OM, I'LL BE HOME SOON. Don't believe everything you read on the Internet."

Four AM. I got a few hours of sleep, but my troubles chased me down. It's ten in Ireland, though, and Morgan bought me a calling card when we went shopping.

Mom's voice is frantic, angry. She's demanding things I can't give her. Demanding I come home immediately, demanding I tell the police they're wrong about me.

Wish I could help you. Seriously.

"Mom, I'm trying. Trust me. I want to come home more than anything in the world, I —"

There's a series of knocks on my hotel room door. No one seems willing to leave me alone.

"Mom, listen, I have to go. I'll call you again later, I promise. Mom, someone is at the door. I love you." Not sure if she hears me through her own rebuttal, but I hang up anyway.

There's another set of knocks as I stumble to the door and open it.

It's Morgan. Black blazer over a charcoal dress, perfectly composed. Nude makeup lacquered; all paradox. "Get dressed," she says. "We're going to see someone."

Suddenly aware that I'm only wearing a pair of boxers. I watch her notice this, but nothing registers. Not embarrassed, or impressed, or laughing.

"Okay. Who are we going to see?"

Morgan doesn't answer me. "Knock on my door when you're ready," she says, then turns and leaves.

The door shuts, cool night extinguished with it.

I get dressed, use the toothbrush and razor she bought me. My new wardrobe hangs in my closet—better than what I wore before.

She picked up a thousand dollars of clothes, and she paid for them like it was an afterthought.

Once I'm dressed, I grab my phone. Earlier, I turned notifications off, since the texts are constant at this point. Another fifty in the past six hours.

I tap the screen. Today's messages start decent enough. Some from Eric—I like Eric, we played soccer together. The first two sound normal, asking if I can talk, if I'm okay. Then he asks why I did it.

There's three from Anna. She's sweet, a pretty redhead. The sentences are perfectly crafted, with immaculate punctuation and spelling. And, they are mostly different ways of promising I'll burn in hell for all eternity.

Then, there's a sharp decline. The rest of the messages are from numbers that aren't in my phone, people I probably never met or spoke with.

And they are bile. Words beaten with sledgehammers then sent tottering at me, suffering misshapen things. All capitalized, misspelled, misused. Shambling, tortured language.

Torture me. Castrate me, burn me with hot irons. Brutalize my mother in front of me, murder my father, hope I get raped in prison daily. A litany of curses from four dozen voices, some howling discordant melody.

Dinosaur minds, cold and dumb and certain.

The door opens; Morgan stands in the frame.

I stare up at her, wet-eyed. "Sorry, I just—my phone."

"Stop looking at it. Come with me."

I follow her out of my motel room and across the night. She flows over the parking lot, long skirt swaying around hips. The single streetlight shines down on a rose red Cadillac, maybe ten years old, a sedan with clean angles like medieval armor. The lights blink in recognition as she presses the unlock button, then we're inside. The engine rumbles to life with the twist of a key.

She takes us into downtown Port Lavaca, down Main Street. We don't see another car the entire way. The shop windows are deep ebony, stop signs and mail boxes cast in steep shade by the occasional street lamp.

None of these shops ever seem crowded, even in the daytime. Pet groomer, refrigerator repair, bullshit trinket shop, shoe restorer. The last few things you can't get done at one of those super stores, the stores people actually shop at.

A traffic light turns red, and Morgan slows to a halt. "My sponsor wants to meet you," she says quietly. "I don't know for sure what will happen."

"Sponsor?"

She nods. "My benefactor. The guy who makes this possible."

"You mean faking your death?"

The question floats restlessly around the car. The light turns green, and Morgan gently brings us up to speed. Even now, with no one around, she obeys every traffic law, and I never see her go past the limit.

"I can't help you unless he agrees you're right for it."

"Right for what?"

Again, no answer.

Painted storefronts transform into an old neighborhood, streetlights making shadow puppets of low-hanging tree limbs. The bay comes into view at the end of the road, black and glistening.

Morgan turns toward Port Lavaca's marina. A ragtag armada bobs there: some shrimp boats, one decrepit yacht, and a neighborhood's worth of house boats. Some of these have lights on, and I see silhouettes cast through the yellow glow within portholes. Shadow theater of the forlorn.

She parks in the gravel lot beside the docks. A row of wooden posts connected by thick ropes marks the edge of the lot; from there, a ten foot drop down to the gulf.

We get out. Morgan retrieves a small flashlight from her purse, and twists the top so it beams to life. I follow her through the gravel parking lot, rocks grinding beneath our feet. Then I'm on the old pier, and can feel the boards sway as waves throw themselves at the pillars and are broken.

The dock is broken into sections, each long pier leading to a dozen boats. From down here, this little floating village is more alive than it seemed. Somewhere, Tejano music plays softly.

Televisions whisper from cracked windows, and a dirty looking man slumbers on the deck of what barely qualifies as a raft.

I follow the flashlight over cords of rope, a dead seagull and the mangled cardboard remains of a box of beer. At the end of the pier sits a houseboat that's not particularly distinct from its neighbors. Blue and white, with the words "La Vittoria" painted on the side in faded cursive. It seems more like a house than a boat; two small rooms nailed to a shallow hull. An iron pipe rises from the center, and smoke drifts out.

Morgan stops outside the boat and raises her hands to the door. "This is it," she says. "Think before you talk."

I nod, but do not move. The white door of the boat shifts gently in the water, and the world is so dark in contrast that I'm hypnotized. Just me and the door; the rest of the universe ceases to exist.

"Inside," Morgan clarifies. "You need to go inside."

With one hand on the wooden post the boat is tied to, I step aboard, walking carefully over the wet wooden slats until I'm standing before the door.

I knock twice, quietly.

"Come in," a voice says. Friendly, an older man's voice.

I twist the knob, push. It opens easily, but with a creak.

Inside, an elderly man sits beside an iron stove. There are no electric lights, and so the chamber is cast in an orange glow, silhouettes constantly shifting as the fire flickers. The stove clads the blaze in a suit of black armor—a pipe acts as chimney and reaches through the roof and beyond.

The man wears a white button-down shirt and red tie. A bowler cap sits in his lap, and his right hand rests across the brim. The sleeves of his shirt are rolled up around his forearms, and a dark tattoo snakes down his wrist to the edge of his hand. In that hand is a small, square glass of an amber liquid.

He looks to be in his sixties, with silver hair buzzed down to his scalp. As he leans to the side to welcome me, his rocking chair tilts back. An identical, empty chair sits across from him.

"Come in," he repeats, calm smile on his face. "Have a seat." He taps his middle, ring and pinky finger against the glass of liquor as he speaks. When his ring finger connects, his wedding band clinks—the result is a hushed drumbeat, two thumps around a high hat.

I move slowly, and hold the sides of the wooden rocking chair as I lower myself down.

"You're Sean Reilly?" he asks.

I pause and he smiles, then speaks: "Bet you hear that a lot. I already know who you are, of course. Most everyone who asks you that knows it's true, but they want you to admit it. They want you to agree you're the entity they need to hold responsible."

"Was wondering why I hear that so much," I say good-naturedly. "What should I call you?"

"You should call me Mr. Banks," he says.

"Okay, Mr. Banks. How are things?" I plant my feet on the floor, so that as the boat rocks against the waves, the chair remains balanced.

"Things are good, Sean. Would you like some scotch? Islay, a single malt. Aged in a cave in Scotland for twenty-one years."

I hesitate, then: "Yeah, sure."

He cracks a grin and picks up a glass identical to his own from the floor near his chair. The bottle is in his other hand, and he's poured an inch of auburn fluid into the vessel. Mr. Banks hands this to me.

"No ice, I'm afraid," he says.

I take a sip. It's strong, more sensation than flavor, just the chemical burn of alcohol. I immediately feel a tiny bit more relaxed.

"I like ghost stories, Sean," he says. "Not scary stories, necessarily, but stories about ghosts. Are you a fan?"

I think about this for a moment, stopping to take another sip. This one is easier, like the first drink burned away most of my taste buds.

"Not particularly."

"Let's see if I can get you interested." He uncrosses his legs then leans in his chair, which rocks back treacherously far. "All cultures write about ghosts. It's called a universal symbol—there aren't many things that all cultures share, but this is one of them. All through history, pretty much everyone thinks something happens after you die."

Mr. Banks scratches his beard. "Not all ghosts are scary, you know. It's just like someone's soul, the same thing. In those old paintings, the ghost is shown as a vapor image of themselves, looking exactly the same, otherwise. Not evil, necessarily."

He takes a sip of scotch, rolls it around his mouth, then swallows.

"Suppose it's true, that someone becomes a ghost after they die, just an invisible version of themselves flying around. He sees his body get buried, all his stuff is given away. Everyone he knows will cry and believe he's dead. So, where does that leave our ghost? He's still the same person, after all, the same person and the same mind. But he's not, at the same time. He's something new, and separate, and the life he knew is gone. So, what is he?"

"Alive," I say.

Mr. Banks takes another sip of his scotch. A log snaps and tumbles deeper into the stove.

Now his voice is low and serious: "When I extend a policy to you, it will be under a condition which I can only express here in this room today, but that you must follow precisely. You must write a suicide note in which you take credit for killing Kayla McPherson, and write that you lied about Kayla faking her death. You must say that you invented Jack Vickery."

I open my mouth, but only cough out half a word.

He rises. So do I, almost automatically. "Thank you for your time," he says. Mr. Banks points toward the door with an open hand.

I find myself outside. Morgan is on the dock, grinning.

11. Plea

THE TAXI DRIVER gives me eighty-seven dollars of Morgan's money back in change; I hand him a five dollar bill as a tip. He's cheered up a little, since my last ride with him. He's probably Port Lavaca's only cabbie.

I'm here to meet the public defender—but before I can do that, something has been weighing on my mind. I take my phone from my pocket, and withdraw my wallet. There's a scrap of paper stuffed between a few dollar bills; I take it out and enter the digits into my phone.

Couldn't call him from the motel room, not when Morgan might be listening. I don't know how Cole fits in yet.

It rings four times before someone answers.

"Cole?" I ask. "You there?"

"Yeah, I'm here. Who is this?" He sounds annoyed.

"Sean Reilly."

I look back and forth across the street, as though I expect Morgan to be watching. She is not.

"You're out of prison," Cole notes. "That's good."

"Yeah. I wouldn't last long in there. Listen, I'm about to talk to my attorney. Is there anything you can tell me that would help? You find anything about Jack, yet?"

"I'm still looking. Listen, who bailed you out?" he asks, voice tinny over the little cell phone speaker.

"A friend of my father." The lie comes easily.

"Is that right?" he asks. "And she's staying in the room next to yours?"

"How did you know that?" I ask. "Were you following me?"

"Listen, Sean, I just don't want you to fall in with the wrong crowd. I'm worried about you. What can you tell me about her?"

I turn, scan the street. An old truck, green body and red hood, passes slowly.

"Nothing. She's a friend of my father's," I insist.

"Come on, Sean. Your parents didn't even know you were out."

"What? You talked to my mom and dad? Who are you?"

"Tell me about her, Sean. I can help you."

"Find Jack. That's how you're supposed to help me, remember? Look, I'm hanging up. Don't call me."

And with the tap of a button, he's gone. Suddenly feeling exposed. He called my parents, he's watched me—why?

I stand still for a moment, waiting to see if he calls back. He does not, and after a minute in the sun, I decide to continue to the attorney's office.

I'm embarrassed to realize my lawyer's office is in a strip mall—acupuncture, pet groomer, nail salon, and the public defender's office. The plastic blinds covering his window are half-broken, and the little slats reveal a dark, cluttered office.

A bell tied to the door jingles as I enter. Hot in here, with no air flow. Got to be eighty, at least.

This room must have desks, filing cabinets and chairs—it's hard to say, because every available surface is covered in stacks of paper, loose binders and overflowing Bankers boxes.

"Hello?" I call.

"Back here," a man's voice answers from further in the office.

I follow the sound to a flimsy door in the back. I open it to find an even smaller, more cluttered sanctuary within the office—the mess outside is only spillage from this room.

A man in a navy blue blazer hunches over a small desk. A pyramid of cardboard boxes, each brimming with red binders and manila folders, is erected behind him.

"Hey," I say. "Nice to meet you."

The public defender's short brown hair is gelled straight up, though some of the congealed spikes are thinner and shorter than others, and a small patch near the back of his scalp is bare. Little black glasses rest on his nose, perched over stubble and a worried frown.

"I'm Tony Jackson. Are you Sean Reilly?" he asks, standing up from his desk, then putting a hand down to stop a stack of papers from sliding to the floor. With the documents tamped down, he extends his left hand for me to shake awkwardly with my right.

"Starting to wish I wasn't," I tell him.

"What?" He cocks his head nervously.

"Starting to wish I wasn't Sean Reilly," I explain.

"Oh. Yes, of course. Have a seat," he says, motioning toward the chair that rests opposite his desk.

I sit.

He spends a long moment looking at me, hands folded in front of his face, fingers interlocked. "Sean, I spent all morning reviewing your case. I've even been on the phone with the district attorney."

"So, how are we going to fix this?"

Mr. Jackson seems to deflate, shoulders dropping a notch. "It may not be a case of 'fixing it,' Sean, but I'm open to ideas. I want to work with you to give this the best outcome we can. But, let me lay out the facts as they see them, and maybe that will help manage your expectations." He holds up three fingers, ticking them off as he finishes each sentence. "During your interview, you admitted to lying to the police about whether or not Kayla wore a life jacket. Second, you admitted to siphoning gas out of the jet ski—given she turned up dead, that alone is enough to make you an accessory to murder. And then there are the drain plugs they found in your closet. You told everyone who would listen you don't know what those are."

"I don't know what those are! What, they stop the jet ski from sinking? Why would they even make it an option to pull them out? Why would you want that?"

"Sean, you told them you planned to make it look like Kayla drowned. Why wouldn't you pull the drain plugs out? Why do you keep lying about them?"

"I didn't do it! Look, there's a guy named Jack Vickery. He told her how to do everything, he pulled out the drain plugs, snuck into my room and put them there."

"Why is there no evidence of a break-in?" His hands are flat on the desk, eyes gazing over rectangular glasses and at me.

"I don't know, maybe Jack did a good job. It's not a bank vault —I was gone all morning, at the beach."

Mr. Jackson looks down at the papers on his desk. "Sean, as far as the police are concerned, Jack Vickery doesn't exist."

I sit for a moment.

"He's using a fake name," I say. "He must be. I told them where his house is, didn't they check?"

"The house is empty, Sean. We need evidence to prove anything we say, otherwise no one will believe it. Do you know what his real name might be? Where we could find Mr. Vickery?"

"I don't know," I say, rising from my chair. The force of my standing shoves it away, and the four legs scratch across the threadbare carpet. "He's hiding, obviously, because he killed Kayla."

Mr. Jackson leans back. "Sean, please, calm down. I'm trying to help you. Like I said, I talked to the district attorney. He's willing to offer you a plea bargain."

I reach back and pull the chair to me, then sit down. "What's that?"

"It's when you and the prosecutor come to an agreement, and avoid a trial. The district attorney does it to save time and money."

"Okay—what's my part of the agreement?"

The public defender takes a deep breath. "Second degree murder. Thirty years," he says.

"What?" I jump out of my chair again. It falls back, turning over a stack of loose papers on a nearby cabinet. The pages rain to the ground.

He says nothing; all I hear is the sound of paper hitting the floor, and my pulse pounding in my ears.

"You're saying all I need to do to avoid going to prison, is agree to go to prison for most of my life?"

"Sean, listen—I'm trying to be realistic, here. What this will do is guarantee you don't get the death penalty."

I put my head in my hands, fingers pressed over my eyes. "I just want to go home. I'll go to college in Ireland, I don't care. Please, get me out of here."

"They aren't going to let you leave, Sean."

I look up. "I won't survive prison. I got assaulted the first time I walked into the hall, do you know what they'll do to me? I want a trial, then. That's what happens if I don't accept the bargain, right?"

"Sean, we can certainly do that. I'll go to trial for you. But what are you going to say? Are you going to blame everything on someone who, as far as we can prove, doesn't exist? What about the lies you admitted to telling? Why did you tell them?"

I rub my hand across my forehead, eyes and cheek. "I don't know. Do you just suck at this? There's got to be a better plan. Thirty years?" My voice breaks as I say the number.

"Sean," he says, voice stern. "Listen to me. It's not the worst possible outcome. You being put to death is the worst possible outcome. Sometimes, life isn't about what's fair. Life is about limiting the damage you're facing, it's about picking the best option available to you in your situation. I'm not telling you we can't go to trial, believe me, I'm not. But if you go to trial, you might get the death penalty. Since we don't have any evidence, and there's a lot of circumstantial evidence stacked against you, they might try for first degree murder. You need to do what you can to save your own life. That plea bargain guarantees you will get to be an old man, that you'll be free again someday."

He smooths the papers on his desk. "Now," his voice is softer, "I understand your being emotional. This is a big deal; we're talking about the rest of your life. But, we have to take this one step at a time, all right? Just stay focused on what you can do now."

As my anger washes away, I'm left with the fear and depression that birthed it. I put my head between my knees, hands across my neck. There's a shiver inside of me, a maddening vibration that jerks and bucks when I move, knocking against my spine, my heart. The quarter in the dryer, spinning heads to tails.

"If I agree to take the plea bargain, what happens?" I ask the floor.

"I call the district attorney and tell him you want to play ball. He'll get you the agreement; once you sign it, we'll all meet at the courthouse, and then you'll go to prison for thirty years," he says. "If you do well, you might get parole after fifteen."

"When would I have to sign it?" Still staring at my shoes.

"The sooner the better," the lawyer says. "They can retract the offer any time they want, so it's better not to make them wait."

"And the plea is the best thing to do, right?" I ask. The world spins around the point between my feet.

"I don't know the answer to that, Sean. I'm telling you that the plea bargain is the only one hundred percent chance you have for escaping execution. Anything else you decide to do, there's a chance they will execute you. At any rate, there's a pretty good chance you'll get more than thirty years."

I make a decision. I look up and lock eyes with the attorney; the spinning stops. "I want to see it. Tell them to send the plea to the motel. I'll sign it soon; I need to write some letters, maybe see my parents, if they get here in time."

I stand up. "Stall them a little, please. This could be my last day or two of freedom."

"Okay, Sean. I'll try to buy some time," he says quietly. "I'll fax the agreement to the motel where you're staying, okay?"

I stand up and walk out of his cluttered den, then the outer office. The door is warm in my hands; shades rattle as I push my way outside.

The dim workplace gives way to the sun, bone-pale orb in the sky. Its light gathers and reflects from the pavement, windows and windshields, brilliance culminating in a bursting flash on my unadjusted eyes.

12. What you know about dying

I CAST LONG SHADOWS as I walk between streetlights. I couldn't sleep, or think, or anything, so I am trying to cure my paralysis with a stroll alongside Port Lavaca's only highway, which connects to my motel. The high school's football stadium looms on my left, a monolithic structure. It is metal and cement rising from the surrounding coastlands, a part of the creeping industrial tumor that stretches from the refineries.

There's some sort of event going on. I can hear it already—the strum of whole chords on an acoustic guitar, amplified over loudspeakers. Trucks fill the gravel field that acts as a parking lot; the rocks grind under my feet with each step. Dull gray aluminum stands are filled on one side by a host of bodies, pale legs jutting from shorts, feet rubbing up against calves to wipe mosquitoes away.

I walk around, past a chain link fence that separates the field from the parking lot. High school students and their parents stand side by side, arms wrapped around shoulders and waists, mom's hair sprayed curls pressed to daughter's straightened bangs. Each clutches a white candle pushed through a plastic cup. The flames dance, tiny and bright beneath each chin.

I stop, hook my fingers around the chain link fence, and watch through the gaps. A teenage boy with a guitar stands midfield, singing something sweet. Happy music under lyrics about angels. Wet faces press to sleeves because hands clutching one another are unable to clear away tears.

The song ends. A girl steps up to the microphone, sniffs wetly.

"Kayla was my lab partner in eleventh grade," she begins. I don't hear the rest, because I'm just understanding what this is.

A candlelight vigil for Kayla. A memorial service, because they know she's dead. A stadium full of people who probably think I murdered her.

Who knows what they'll do if they see me. Christ.

And, there's so many people; the emotion is so genuine. Kayla's death made an impact. There are probably a thousand people in the stands. And most of these must be acquaintances; they didn't spend time with Kayla while she lived. I'd have seen them.

But, they're coming to terms with the fact that Kayla is gone forever. That each little memory of her, even the passing ones that seem insignificant, will now be buried—only to be revisited on occasion as remnants of something past, something dead.

Stranger, still: Kayla planned on being here to watch this. This moment, this memorial, would occur even if everything went according to plan—even if Kayla still lived. Her actually being dead is the least important part of the entire process.

So, where does she really live? How you can bury something that could still be alive, unless the thing you're burying isn't what you thought it was at all?

The breeze rolls one of the white candles, half melted, against the fence. I lean down and pick it up. It fits snugly in my pants pocket.

When I arrive back at the motel, I go to the front office. A middle-aged Mexican woman sits behind the desk.

"Is there a fax for me? I'm Sean Reilly, in room 14."

She huffs, pushing her arms against the counter to roll her chair across the office. A set of documents rest in a cardboard box-top. The office manager picks them up, wrinkles her nose at the pages.

"These yours? A..." she hesitates, looking at the top of the page. "A plea bargain?"

I take the papers without answering, and walk silently out of the office.

When I'm a few feet from my room, a door cracks open. A woman's face fills the space: blank slate of a forehead, wide-set blue eyes drinking in what light remains. An interesting face—bizarre, even, but not unattractive.

I stop. "What do you know about dying?" I ask her.
"Everything," she answers, smiling.

13. Corpse road

YESTERDAY MORNING, I woke up with nothing. I've still got all of it.

Thirty hours awake. It's six AM, and I'm walking toward the inevitable. More precisely, I'm walking down an empty suburban street to Kayla's house. There's something I must deliver.

Nice neighborhood. Lots of trees, well-kept lawns, no cars parked on the street. Basketball goals for the kids, luxury cars for mom and dad. Here and there, a bike tipped over in the lawn, a forgotten toy left undisturbed during the night.

Sweat drips down my cheek, despite the cool morning. The small stub of a white candle rests in my pocket, and I feel it rub on my thigh as I walk. Someone else's burnt out memory of Kayla McPherson.

Can't feel my feet—I only get a slightly dizzy sensation as my head bobs, as though I am disembodied and float to my destination.

Behind it all is the sense that I'm not actually here, and this isn't really happening.

The McPherson home draws near. A house more modest than its neighbors: no stone pillars, no light fixtures drawing a path to the front door. A place I was once welcome.

I'll be arrested immediately if I'm caught here, I know. But, this has to be done. My feet press against the curb and crunch across the grass, slick with dew.

I'm on the doorstep. The vague shape of their living room is outlined through the frosted glass panels of the door. As I lean down, I push against one for balance. A clear handprint is drawn from the morning's cold condensation.

I push a red envelope beneath their door.

And then I walk away. I've got a long way to go, and the sun is just rising.

14. Crossing over

STILL WALKING, except now I'm all the way to the Port Lavaca causeway. Clear day, pale sky, white clouds. No souls walk here, just mine. The heat of the day bleaches the earth clean, scares off even the insects. I do like that about Texan weather—the antiseptic sun.

The bridge shudders every time a car passes, a tiny wobble I never noticed while driving.

A car honks as it moves to avoid clipping my left side. There is only a narrow cement ledge here, not designed for walking on. I'm interrupting the morning commute.

The Gulf of Mexico is about fifty feet below me. Ahead, the bridge slopes upward, to make way for tall vessels. Below that hump in the bridge, the water is carved deep so that ships can move through the channel. I'm heading for the peak.

Another car honks, swerves.

I keep moving, walking at a steady pace, hands in my pockets. Today, a walk is not just a walk, and these are the most difficult steps of my life. My destination is my unmaking.

I count furiously, to keep myself moving. When the fear comes, I concentrate on counting faster, louder, until I shout the numbers internally, and they consume my mind. There is no space for anything else; there can be no space.

The wind snaps across my face, catches my t-shirt and pulls it against my body. Sweltering wind, salted spray. I can feel the fine particles grind on my skin, pull the moisture from my face.

One foot in front of the other. That's my whole world. Walking, and counting. I climb the incline. Soon, my head crests the top of the curve, and I'm here.

And now I can't seem to count loud enough.

It's a hundred foot drop down to the water below. I stand at the apex of the bridge and turn to face the bay, stepping up on the knee-high cement guard that prevents cars from tumbling over the edge.

I look down. I expected a straight drop, but I can see some stone fixtures from the bridge extend a foot or two, maybe ten feet below me. Below that, the brown waters of the gulf. Thick as chocolate milk, constantly clouded from the soft silt that makes the floor of the sea.

My knees bend to hold my balance as another gust of wind hits, pulls me to the left. I stretch out my arms to my sides, fingertips pointing at the horizon. The sun is behind me.

I hear the squeal of tires on road; a car lurches to a stop, and the next truck jerks into the opposite lane, hitting his brakes as well. The cars behind all struggle to brake in time.

I nearly cause an accident. But I just stand on the edge of the world, arms out, unmoving.

A car door opens. I tilt my head to the left. An overweight bald man waves his arms, belly bouncing. He jumps up and down, vying for my attention. More doors open, more concerned strangers get out.

No one gets too close. The shouting drowns within the roar of the wind and the scream of my nerves.

I have counted all the numbers.

Then I turn to look back at the water, and all strength leaves me. I see my destiny a hundred feet below. My knees buckle. I lean over the side, and become dizzy; the world seems to lurch up behind me as I pitch forward.

And I take that moment, bend my knees and push.

Slow cataclysm. I'm airborne. Facing the sky first, watching it spin away, watching the bridge shrink from me, vision tunneling. I am within a moment that divides by half infinitely, accelerating endlessly. Muddy water rushes toward me, and I push my hands in front of my head, forming a spear.

All the force in the world thrusts me into hard darkness. Each molecule of water reacts to my intrusion, and the entire ocean is split to make way for one unwelcome visitor.

Another body for the gulf—Sean Reilly dies today.

15. Gulf

W HAT IS THIS WORLD?
I exist. I must; I am asking this question. I must exist.

If I exist, I must breathe. I know this instinctively—it is beyond thought.

When I start to open my mouth, I feel a pressure on my lips. Pressure that reminds me of something I knew once, something I told myself. Something very important.

Not to breathe. I must not breathe.

I open my eyes; they burn, I see nothing. I realize: I am underwater. I am in the gulf.

And then I feel everything. Pain overtakes me, centered on my right knee. I know immediately my leg is broken; when I tug at my thigh, pain sears my nerves. I can't move my foot at all, though I can feel the weight of it.

My knee is out of socket. I'm acutely aware of this because when water tugs at my shoe, it pulls the dislocated joint further away, into my muscle and skin. This is agony.

I spread my arms, fingers extended, and fill my hands with ocean, pull myself through. The pain in my leg explodes; I scream silently and the brine fills my mouth. So salty it's painful, like acid on my tongue.

I stretch my arms forward and pull again. Must get to the other side of the bridge, must get out of eyesight. Then I can take a breath.

That is the plan. There is a plan, there's a reason I'm here. It comes back to me as I swim.

But mostly, the plan is: hope.

Just a little concussion, a broken knee. At least I am alive. Morgan showed me that cliff divers jump from twice as high and live. But, they practiced.

Another armful of water, and I spiral to my back, forcing open my eyes to see the dark outline of the bridge overhead. I swim in its shade, looking up through light made fluid by the curves of the ocean. I push my mouth above the water and take a breath. My lungs beg for more, but I dive back down, pump my arms, continuing to move parallel to the bridge, out of sight.

Grab water, pull. Grab, pull.

Exhaustion sets in before I'm halfway to the shore, but as I cross the channel, the water becomes shallow. I can grip handfuls of sand, kick with my working leg off the sediment, and propel myself with ease. When my lungs burn uncontrollably, when I feel them crackle and strain, I lift and allow for a small breath of air. I only hope the murky water hides my movement.

I'm at the other end, in water so shallow I can't stay submerged. I slide up on the shore, knee burning in pain, and look back at the causeway which stretches across the bay. My stomach churns as I imagine my fall.

I survived. That's something.

I turn onto my chest, then pull myself forward with my arms and elbows. The sand clings to my shirt, which sticks to my skin. Port Lavaca's shell-pocked coast lays before me, a flat marsh extending behind.

A red Cadillac is parked on the beach. A figure in a blue hoodie and jeans stands next it, arms crossed, hood pulled down. I know this is Morgan by the brown bangs which whip in the breeze.

I press my palms into the shells and pull my good leg up to my chest. Push, push, careful now—I rise. My broken leg hangs limp on the ground, an inch longer than my other. The pain is unbearable; so much that it radiates to my skull, vibrating down to my teeth like the end of a tuning fork that's been struck.

The figure in the blue hoodie jogs close, feet kicking up sand which gets caught in the wind and blown away. Morgan stands on the side of my broken leg and wraps an arm around me. "Lean on me," she says, voice strained. "We need to hurry."

She takes a step, and I lean on her shoulders while moving my good leg. Morgan acts as my crutch as we hobble up the beach toward her car.

When we're almost there, I see someone else in the car, riding shotgun. The outline of his hood is obvious through the window. Alarms ring, though I'm so exhausted and in such pain that I can't process what is happening.

Morgan leads me to the rear of the car and opens the trunk. "Get in," she commands.

I stare harder at the person in the passenger seat.

I can't. "I can't," I say. My brain isn't working: too much everything. Too much pain, exhaustion, and adrenaline.

"You have to," she growls. "They'll see you and it'll be over for all of us."

"But that's Jack," I say, nodding toward Jack, who sits in the passenger seat, smiling behind his red hood. "Jack is in the car."

16. Are you Sean Reilly?

H OT, MUSTY, DARK. The rough fabric of the trunk's interior scrapes against my cheek, and my neck aches from the awkward angle I'm forced into. I lay flat on my side, with my weight on my good leg.

Morgan makes a sharp right turn, and I struggle for balance, instinctively pushing against the side of the trunk with my broken leg.

I bite the crook of my arm, throat flexing in a silent howl. My knee dangles, ruined thing, from my thigh. I can feel the tissue, inflamed and angry, furiously sensitive to every disturbance. The muscles seem torn, disconnected, and I sense the bottom half of my leg is connected to the top half only by my skin.

When the car straightens out, a white waxy cylinder rolls against my face. It's the candle from Kayla's vigil, fallen from my pocket. The things we have in common.

Except she stayed in the gulf, and I crawled out. Sean Reilly is dead, but I'm still here, and I'm in pain.

All thanks to Jack. Jack, who almost certainly killed Kayla, slashed her throat and tried to hide the body in the ocean. Set me up to look guilty. Wanted me to be executed for his crime.

Jack's crime, which I confessed to. His crime that I wrote a suicide note claiming I committed, a note that says Jack Vickery is a creation of my guilty mind. A note I put under the McPherson's door this morning.

But, he's not a creation of my mind. He's sitting in the car, and for some reason Morgan is allowing it.

The front wheels pop over a pothole, and I brace with my good leg and two arms as the rear wheels follow. I'm jolted from position; the pain is tremendous, and the journey nauseating. Just pitch black, all signals coming through the roll of the car, the mechanical conversation between engine and transmission.

After ages of bumps and turns, the car settles into a straight and steady path. A highway, maybe.

The fabric from my drenched clothes is harsh and stiff as the seawater evaporates, leaving behind a layer of salt and sand that grates against my skin. I listen to the clutch engaging, the gear shifting, the throttle opening. We roll forward, and I roll backward. We stop, and I roll forward. Each movement brings fresh torment.

We drive for hours. My only companions are the pain, and the slow-dawning realization of what I've done.

"Are you Sean Reilly?"

How many times have I been asked that, in the past week? A dozen? Every attorney, cop, and consul I've come across?

For the rest of my life, if anyone asks me that, my only response will be to deny it—deny it and run. Sean Reilly is no more. He jumped to his death after leaving a suicide note at the McPherson home. So, who am I?

The car stops; the engine dies. Doors open, then slam shut.

I roll over so that I'll be facing whoever opens the trunk. A key is inserted; the latch releases. As the lid opens, the sun beams through and dazzles me, leaving me momentarily blind.

Morgan stands, one arm up high, resting on the open trunk lid. The sun is angled directly behind her head, so a glaring halo shines from behind, leaving her a darkened shadow by contrast.

The blue hood is tight around her hair, and that impenetrable calm radiates from her face. The same wall; that surface which all of my unanswered questions bounce from.

"We can rest here," she says.

"Where's Jack?"

She extends a hand. "Jack is gone, don't worry about him. Worry about you, first. The police are probably looking for you, and you're not exactly mobile."

I take her hand and pull; testing that she can support my weight. Morgan stands steady. I position the working portion of my body around my broken knee, disturbing the wound as little as possible.

"I'm going to need a wheelchair," I say. "And a doctor."

"I'm working on it." Morgan pulls a strand of hair from her cheek, tucking it back into the hood. "For now, you get a room. We can't risk a trip to the emergency room yet. They might be watching."

Fantastic. With her help I sit up in the trunk, good leg hanging out while the broken knee rests inside. I feel faint; the blood seems to drain from my head. I lean back, rest against the car. I see we're parked behind a long, white brick building spotted with a dozen brown doors, and there's no one in sight.

"Where's Jack?" I ask again, breath coming in ragged gasps.

"Come on," Morgan says. She withdraws a key from her purse; it's attached to a rectangular keychain that reads *Comfort Suites*. She pushes this into the brown door nearest the car and twists, then pulls it open.

Another musty hotel room, like the last. Morgan steps to me, gets on my bad side and kneels under my arm. Can feel as the brittle material of my shirt resists her; bits of salt flake away.

We hobble into the room. "The bathroom," I say, when she stalls beside the bed. She nods, and we limp a bit further. When we reach the cramped sink and shower, there's no room to assist me. I cling to door frames and handicap hand-railings, propelling myself forward. I sink back into the hard porcelain bathtub, letting my broken leg rest elevated over the side.

"It's okay," I mumble to Morgan as she stands in the door frame, watching. "I'll shout when I need to get out, okay?"

She nods, thumbnail perched between lips. After a long stare, she shuts the door.

I struggle to pull the salt-stiff shirt from my body, knocking over the little plastic-wrapped bar of soap and bottle of shampoo, sending them rattling around the dry tub. When the shirt is pulled free, silt shakes off and into my hair and eyes.

I reach and turn on the shower. The water rains down cold at first, and I bear the shock until heat slowly comes. I lean back, feeling it soak my socks, jeans and boxers.

What the hell have I done?

I spend the better part of an hour removing my pants: a multistage process that brings smoldering waves of pain at every step.

Once the last of my clothes are in a filthy pile on the bathroom floor, I can inspect my knee. It's a deep purple, swollen and bloated; the flesh looks oxygen-starved and near death. The ball of my knee rests below and in front of the space it belongs, an obscene bulge. From the middle of my shin down to my foot, though, things seem normal enough.

I'll need a doctor, for sure. I broke my wrist once, and they put me through surgery, put pins in my body to hold everything in place while it healed. I can't just wrap this up and limp around: it'll never work again.

I lean back in the tub, pulling my broken knee in with me. With it floating, the pain lessens to a dull throb—enough so that my exhaustion outweighs the pain, and I fall asleep.

17. To be dead

I'M AWOKEN BY KNOCKING on the bathroom door. I am spilled uselessly into the near-empty tub. My broken knee is numb and black, sitting obstinately in an inch of bathwater, daring me to try and move.

I reach for a towel that's folded on a rack overhead, dragging the thin cloth down and spreading it over my lap. The material soaks up the cooling water and clings to my skin.

"Come in," I say.

Morgan pushes open the door and focuses immediately on my mangled leg. Her eyes go wide; she turns away for a moment, making a disgusted sound. Then she turns back, eyes fixed on the wall above me. "Your knee is broken," she notes, expression slack.

"Could have been my neck," I say. "Come on, could you help me up?"

She steps in, and despite my general exhaustion, I can't help but realize I'm basically nude in front of this attractive woman.

I reach out; Morgan wraps both her hands around my wrist. "Slow," I warn, as my broken knee begins to shift. "Slow!" I shout again at no one in particular, as the pain mounts.

My right arm holds the towel loosely to my body; the left is in Morgan's hands. I rise from the tub, pushing myself upright with my good leg. Rather than stepping out, I sit on the edge, lifting my bad leg over.

She pulls me up again, and we hobble together to the bedroom. When we reach the bed, I fall backward, pulling myself up on a nest of pillows so that I'm sitting upright. I bring the towel with me, then replace it with the bed's comforter.

"Thank you," I mumble. "Now, what the hell was Jack doing? Where is he?"

"Forget about Jack," she says.

"He murdered Kayla, and I took the blame for it."

"That's right," she says. "You took the blame for it. If you bring Jack to the police now, after your suicide note and fake death, you think they're going to believe you? At the very least, you will be on trial for murder, and in prison for faking your death to escape that trial in the first place."

"But he's the real killer!"

"Sean Reilly is dead. Anyone finds out you're him, it's straight to prison, probably for a long time. Which, I might remind you, is what would happen anyway if we didn't help out."

This quiets me. I wrack my brain, but can't imagine a situation where the police arrest Jack and set me free. Not after what's happened.

So I just stare at the ceiling.

"I got you some things," Morgan says, lifting a shopping bag from the room's sole chair and setting it on the bed.

"This doesn't seem real," I mumble. "I keep thinking about that —Sean Reilly is dead."

"You're more than a name," Morgan tells me. "You're not really dead."

"It doesn't feel that way right now," I say, turning to the curtains, which glow dimly from the sunlight. There's a knot of dread in my throat, and I swallow it back.

"You need to sleep. This is all I've got, but I'm going to get you something stronger when I have a chance." She pulls a bottle of pills from her purse, then shakes four of the little blue orbs into the palm of her hand, and extends it. I let the pills fall into mine before tossing them into my mouth and drinking from the bottled water that follows.

18. After life

SOMETIME IN THE MORNING, I begin coughing. In my drugged slumber, I forget what's happened, and my body convulses with each ragged breath—this moves my broken leg, and so I'm launched into the waking world with a shock, ripped from my dreams by new pain.

Good morning, me.

I peel back the blankets and inspect the damage. From my lower thigh down to my shin, the muscle is swollen and dark. The skin over the injury is a deep purple, but my foot is a normal color, which seems promising. I can even curl my toes, if I focus through the hurt.

Still, I'm not going anywhere.

No more cell phone, as Morgan insisted I leave it untouched in my bedroom. People don't bring their phones to a suicide, apparently. There's nothing to occupy me but the small television perched on the dresser across from the bed. With a flick of the remote, it comes to life.

I flip channels until I find a local station. Five minutes of the weather, a block of commercials, then the news.

Port Lavaca is reeling. Yesterday, Sean Reilly, the 18-year-old Irish exchange student who was arrested as a suspect for the murder of Kayla McPherson, jumped to his death. He was released on a $50,000 bond just two days prior. A suicide note left under the door of the McPherson household includes the message 'I'm sorry for everything, but most of all, I'm sorry for Kayla's death.'

The camera flips to a different reporter, who stands in the driveway of a suburban neighborhood. I recognize the garage door—he's outside the McPherson's home. Ruthless bastards.

The McPhersons aren't shown, but a boy I went to school with is standing in the doorway. The microphone is presented to his face.

I knew Sean, you know. I couldn't imagine him doing something like this. You know what really makes me sick? He came out and helped us search for Kayla when she first went missing, stayed there all night—and the whole time, he knew what happened. He killed her!

—Why do you think he did it?

He must have been a really sick individual, that's all I can say on camera.

And I played soccer with this guy. We were friends.

The news segment continues, and I'm glued to it. It's like watching one's house burn down; tragic, but mesmerizing. Becoming undone.

The screen changes to a memorial for Kayla at the high school, a stack of crosses and stuffed animals. Students stand beside it and are interviewed.

He took someone very special from us. Sean Reilly was troubled, you could see it in his eyes.

You could?

He had this vacant stare, like you never knew what was going on in his head. I never trusted him.

You didn't?

Sean just kept to himself most of the time, he didn't have a lot of friends. Kind of a loner.

Hey, asshole, I had plenty of friends. I was a fairly popular novelty. I only needed to endure two Lucky Charms jokes a day to keep everyone aware of my existence.

Not that there's anything I can say to that, now. Don't have any friends, anymore. In fact, I can never talk to any of those people ever again. Sean Reilly is all theirs, now.

So, who am I? When I was born, at least my parents were waiting on me, waiting to love me. Now, I don't even have them. I'm alone.

It's like a silence inside me. A dead quiet.

It's just me in this world, and I hate it.

Morgan opens my door. Her knee-length dress sports thick black and white horizontal stripes.

"Hey," she says quietly. "How are you feeling?"

I look away. "My knee hurts."

"I brought better drugs," she says, holding up an orange prescription medicine bottle. She tosses this on my chest, and I let it roll to the floor, rattling all the way.

"Cheer up," she commands.

"Subtle."

"Moping doesn't suit you. I thought you'd be able to handle this."

"I saw them talking about it on the news. Everyone hates me."

"That's not you. You can go on and live your life now. I will teach you how to make money, how to enjoy your new freedom," Morgan says. "They hate something in their heads they tell themselves is Sean Reilly, but it's not you. It never is."

"But that is me! I'm Sean Reilly!"

Morgan reaches into her purse. Her hand reappears with a small blue envelope, the size of a greeting card. She flips this on the bed.

The package is heavy. I peel back the small red sticker that seals the envelope, and pull out the contents.

"A gift from Mr. Banks," she says.

A blue card falls from the envelope to my chest. I pick it up. The words 'United States Social Security Administration,' are stamped in gold lettering, with a nine-digit number printed across the front. Below that, a name: Ryan White.

"I don't want this," I say. "I want to be Sean Reilly. I don't know who Ryan White is." I press my palm into my left temple and slide it down my face. "I'm trying to be positive about this, really, I am. I just don't understand."

Morgan doesn't react, only walks to the sink and examines herself in the mirror.

I look through the rest of the envelope: A birth certificate, credit card, and social security card. Ryan White is nineteen, a year older than me, or would be. I wonder if he was a real person, if anyone misses him. Someone must be missing me.

It hits me—sometime soon, if not already, my parents will be told that I murdered Kayla McPherson, left a note admitting this, and committed suicide by jumping off a bridge.

Morgan told me about this, though. I can't let them know I'm alive, at least not for a while. Not for years.

They love me too much. They'll be my downfall.

My door opens again. Jack enters, hands inside the center pocket of his red hoodie, blue jeans hanging halfway down his ass. I tense, pulling myself up on the bed. My leg burns as I do, reminding me how helpless I am.

"Look at this," Jack says, hand coming up from his pocket with an electronic cigarette, blue tip glowing as he inhales. "A boy without a shadow—that's a beautiful thing. Enjoy it. You're free."

"I lost everything because of you."

"You lost it in a blaze of glory. Sean Reilly died a legend. Kayla's parents will talk about you until they die—Port Lavaca won't ever shut up about their Irish slasher. In fifty years, kids will tell scary stories while their parents drive across that causeway. Let's face it—there's nothing you—" He points at me now, one skeletal finger extended. "—will ever do that makes as big of an impact. You did your shadow justice, and you're better off."

My voice falls low, and I glare at him. "They'll tell stories about something you did. You killed her, didn't you? Then made it seem like I'm guilty, and now you're trying to make me thank you. You're sick. You're subhuman trash."

Jack steps to the front of the bed. I pull the sheets that hide my body closer. I'm still naked, and the room is getting crowded.

Morgan intervenes: "I need you to help me get him into a hospital. He needs surgery. Find me someplace quiet to drop him."

He bites on the plastic cigarette, teeth bared around a smile. "Now I'm supposed to help this ungrateful little shit?" Jack rubs the back of his neck. "Why would I do that?"

"Because I am making you," she tells him.

He faces her, takes a step forward, then stops. Thin arms fall limp. "There's a lot to consider."

"I'm not doing anything with him," I point out.

He grins and I notice a sparse, blond beard stretches from ear to ear. The image of Jack with yellow hair is cringe-worthy.

Jack speaks, though the words sound forced: "No hard feelings, buddy. Don't worry about the past. You're a new man, now."

I address Morgan. "Why are we in the same room as this goddamn psychopath?" My voice is louder than I intend. "I thought I could trust you. You said you wanted to help me; you said we'd been betrayed. I assumed you meant by Jack, but here you are with him."

Jack hacks out a laugh.

Morgan turns to him. "You, leave. Find us a hospital."

He raises both hands again, half bowing, then turns and exits. The door slams against its frame behind him.

Then she faces me, smile gone, all stone mask. "I don't care if you trust me. Personally, I wouldn't either. It is in my best interest to keep you from talking to the police about Jack and I, and what we do. Keeping you close is one way to accomplish that goal. He'd rather kill you, but I'm inclined to turn you into an asset. It's less risky, and I'm not a murderer."

Morgan continues. "From your perspective, you'd be completely screwed if I walked out now. Even if I convince him not to murder you, you'll be trapped here until the cops come, and you will have a lot of explaining to do. So if I were you, for the time being, I'd keep my mouth shut and play along."

19. Then you refuse to speak

FOUR AM, driving down a deserted street in Somewhere, USA. Streetlights rise and set across the night. Thick ferns cast diabolical silhouettes over flat, one-story industrial buildings—half of them corrugated steel, the other half, faded brick. We pass a bus stop; either a homeless man or a bundle of ragged clothes rests on the bench.

"Where the hell are we, anyway?" I'm stretched out across the back seat of Morgan's car as we head to the hospital.

"Louisiana," Morgan answers. "Lake Charles."

A name and a place that don't mean anything to me. This new travel is magic. Jump off a bridge, duck into a trunk, and wake up in a new land.

"Why don't we just get on a plane and go to another country?" Ireland sounds nice this time of year.

"I could," Morgan informs. "You and Jack need photo IDs. Can't fly without them."

Jack speaks: "If you're done telling us how to do what we do best, here's the plan: We're going to Dubois Hospital. Lake Charles Memorial is the best hospital in the area, and it's just a couple miles away. Not much traffic at Dubois, it's older. We'll get you in during the morning shift, we'll pull you out at the shift change that night. If I'm right and that's a dislocation, they aren't going to do too much cutting. You should be conscious within six or seven hours of the operation. Now, can you talk normal?" Jack turns around in the front seat to face me.

"I don't want to talk to you," I tell him. "Morgan, you tell me what to do. I don't want to hear anything out of Jack's mouth."

Jack feigns a hurt expression, leans back and slaps my bad foot. Barely a tap, but the pain is monumental; I inhale sharply, pull back.

"Cut it out, Jack," Morgan says.

He doesn't. "A smart person could see I'm trying to help you out here. You think I'm so bad for killing Kayla—you killed Sean Reilly, how do you feel about that?"

"Because I didn't actually kill anyone," I say. "I'm not really a murderer."

"You killed the shadow, and that's what people miss, that's what they owned. If you accept, like I do, that individual people don't matter much in the scheme of things—that scheme being chaotic in the first place—then we're pretty much equal. I made a lot of people sad someone is dead, and so did you."

I say nothing.

"Now, answer me—can you talk normal?"

"I do talk normal," I tell him.

"I mean, can you talk American." He draws out the word, makes his voice flat. "Without the accent."

I straighten my back, try it out: "Jack Vickery fondles dogs."

I can see Morgan smirk through the rearview mirror.

"It doesn't matter what breed of dog," I say, trying to straighten out my inflections, over-enunciate every syllable. "Big dog, small dog, don't let him near them."

"Please stop," Jack says. "You're going to need to keep your mouth shut while you're inside, hard as that might be. You still sound Irish."

"Why can't Ryan White have grown up in Ireland? Then I won't need to change my voice."

"Because that makes you a rarity; it makes you easy to remember. You need to learn how to think—let's say the police call around, looking to see if anyone with an Irish accent checked into a hospital with injuries like you might get from jumping off a bridge. And that clerk at the hospital says what? 'Oh yeah, I remember him, his name is Ryan White.' And you're still out here telling the world you're Ryan White. They'll find you in a week," Jack informs. "But, if you keep your mouth shut, or give them a fake name, they still have to treat you. It's the law."

"So I'm stealing? From doctors?" Jesus.

He turns and grins. "Yeah, you're stealing—get used to that. You opted out of the civilized world when you decided to shed your shadow. Didn't you read the fine print?"

I don't like that. However, I like the pain in my leg even less. Just want to stop feeling my knee cap roll around, really.

"So these are pointless?" I ask, pulling Ryan's social and birth certificate from the pocket of my jeans.

"Leave them in the car," Jack says. "If they find them, they'll know how to find you. The less record of this, the better. The less record you exist, the better. This world tracks you, it gets hooks in everywhere you go."

I stuff Ryan White's identity into the pocket behind the driver's seat. The hospital comes into view, emergency room entrance adorned with red plastic crosses.

"And how do I get an operation without talking?"

We pull up to the entrance, underneath a two-lane cement awning.

Jack grins. "Have you ever heard the term *aphasia voluntaria?*"

Using the crutches is extremely painful, as my broken leg hangs uselessly, dragging along the floor. My shoelaces are untied, and make a soft scratching sound on the linoleum. I am a macabre installation.

I believe my dangling leg is the reason I'm approached by a nurse before I get halfway to the desk at the end of the emergency room. It is a Monday morning, and the room is empty.

"Let me get a wheelchair," she insists, waving at an orderly who hesitates at the opposite end of the room. "What happened?"

I point at my mouth, shake my head, then make a scribbling motion with my hand.

"You want paper?" she asks.

I nod in agreement. A Hispanic man in scrubs comes from behind with a wheelchair; I lean back in it, gently, letting my mangled leg rest on the ground.

She's back, pen and pad in hand. I take the cheap plastic pen and write on the pad:

I don't talk.

Then:

My knee is broken. I'm in pain.

The nurse leans down to my foot, begins gently rolling my jeans up my leg. Even this makes me recoil in pain, as the slightest touch feels like it shifts an ice pick that's jabbed deep in my bone.

"How did this happen?" she asks.

Fell off my motorcycle, I write.

She looks skeptical.

"You can't talk, or you won't talk?"

I place the tip of the pen on my first message, and make eye contact.

The nurse shakes her head. "We need to lift your foot into the stirrup, so we can wheel you into the operating room. Do you want to lift it, or me?"

I put both hands on the thigh of my injured leg, and lift from here. Lights flash in my eyes; the pain is a shrill ringing in my ears. The job is done.

"Are you allergic to any medication? Write it out," she says.

I'm not allergic to any medication.

"Do you have any identification? What's your name?"

No identification.

20. Hospital bills

WAKING UP IS A GRADUAL PROCESS that begins with my body drifting up from the bottom of a deep blue pool. The pool is perfectly round, and seems bottomless. Cool serenity.

At its base, I have only the faintest awareness of being. Can't remember who I am, or what's brought me here—I only possess a sense of existing. I wonder if this is what it was like moments before I was born.

I rise, slowly, memories flitting past. As I climb, light grows, and thought sharpens. The closer I get to the top, the lonelier I become. The emptier.

Of all that's happened in the past week, the realization I've lost Sean Reilly is the worst. I am a new kind of alone, without even myself to rely on for company.

My nose and mouth push to the surface, skin of water opening to allow my lips past, its slick grip sliding across my face.

I inhale reality.

My eyes open. My leg is wrapped in a complex cast, black plastic with multiple joints and straps. It all feels infinitely better than when I arrived—secure and intact, joint held together by the bindings.

There sits a dense layer of warm foam between myself and my senses, a vibrating golden hum of prescription-grade painkillers. I assume I'm on morphine. Not complaining—this is my first pain-free moment in days.

I lift my hand; I'm plugged in, and needles protrude from my veins. One of these is the syrup drip of comfort. I tug on the tubes, but can't bring myself to remove them. Too heavy; too warm.

A silhouette fills the window in the door, which opens and closes without a sound. I force my eyes open, swallow twice, three times. For some reason, this is difficult.

"What do you need to get out of here?" Morgan asks, voice hushed. Her hair is tucked into a red baseball cap, and a loosely knit sweater drapes across shoulders, faintest outline of her black bra visible through the threads.

"A wheelchair," I mumble.

"A what?"

I swallow, then try again. God, this morphine. "A wheelchair."

Morgan nods, pulls her cap low, and disappears out the door. Moments later she returns, walking backward with a wheelchair in tow.

My rescuer pulls the purse from her shoulder, reaches inside, and withdraws a handful of clothes. A pair of shorts are tossed onto my chest.

I watch them for a moment, slow in my drugged stupor. She sighs, then reaches for the blanket that covers me, ripping it back, exposing me to the air.

Too high to blush. Morgan steps to the end of the bed, holds the shorts open, and slides my feet through. The cast snags several times, and she pulls the fabric free until at last I'm covered.

"Come on. The nurses are changing shifts, we've got to hurry or someone will stop us," she says.

I point at my hand. She grabs the needles and yanks them out; I barely feel it. Little droplets of blood appear in a row on my hand, wet rubies.

Morgan leans forward again, nearness exciting me, and slides a shirt over my head.

"Come on," she says, bringing the wheelchair closer. "Grab the sides. That's right. Give me your leg, I'll set it here. Okay, how is that?"

I can't tell if that hurt or not; everything still feels so wonderful. My cast is elevated on an extended leg rest, then we're moving. She pushes me into an empty hall; a patient snores loudly. Screensavers bounce around otherwise dormant computer monitors.

We're in the elevator, going down. It opens to the first floor. Morgan moves in a hurry, walking fast as she wheels me toward the exit, and we're through, into the tepid Louisiana night.

A red Cadillac sits in the otherwise barren parking lot, waiting for us. Wheels roll smooth over the pavement. We reach the car, and as Morgan opens the door, I see a man jogging out the front of the hospital.

"Goddamnit," Morgan curses.

I struggle to lift myself from the wheelchair, slipping and losing balance. I lurch forward and grasp the seat of the car, clinging to the seatbelt like a mountain climber grabs sturdy roots, pulling myself into the back seat. I turn to check: the man running through the parking lot is wearing the blue uniform of a security guard.

"Jack is supposed to be here. That son of a bitch." She wraps both arms around my legs, lifting and pushing as I pull.

"Just drive," I mumble.

She shuts the door; I'm inside, sprawled over the back seat. Morgan jogs around to the front, opens it, and in a second the engine revs to life. The machine snarls as we race out of the parking lot—the security guard's run breaks to a jog, and his shoulders slump as he settles for grabbing our stolen wheelchair just as it begins to roll across the pavement.

"Sean, I need you to check the pocket where you put your new ID."

I do so, reaching into the pocket behind Morgan's seat, where I put Ryan White's documents. The fabric of the seat itches the little needle pricks in my hand.

"There's nothing in here," I say. The warmth is beginning to fade, and I wonder if I should be as worried as Morgan is.

"Shit. Goddamnit, Jack, you idiot."

"Why would Jack want my ID?"

"Because Jack doesn't have an identity, and that's made him very desperate. It's why he's hiding. Except now, he has yours."

21. Tile

"SO WHAT?" I ask. "It's not like someone asks who you are every day. How bad do you really need ID?"

Morgan looks back from the driver's seat. "Spoken like a teenager. Without ID there are no credit cards, no flights, you can't get anything online, you can't sign up for anything, the list goes on. Any cop ever questions you, there's a chance you'll get arrested. In jail, they'll use fingerprints to start putting together who you are. Eventually, they figure it out. There's only so much you can pay for with cash, and Jack doesn't have any..."

Brakes squeal; I slide forward. Morgan makes a U-turn, then slams down the accelerator; the smell of burning rubber wafts into the cabin.

Streetlights shine on her face in quickening pulses. Between the night and sudden flashes of light, color drains from our world, and Morgan's skin appears porcelain, eyebrows black strokes of a calligrapher's brush, ebony lips pressed into a tight, flat line.

The undercarriage scrapes as we pull into our motel parking lot; Morgan speeds into a parking space so quickly that I flinch, fearing she'll go straight through the building.

"Stay here," she says.

I wait as she storms to the room. Moments later, she returns, folded sheet of paper in one hand.

"Jack stole my stash." Morgan climbs into the driver's seat. The paper is unfolded; it is yellow tinted, a page from the phone book. Her hand clenches the wheel, bending the page. "Jack stole my goddamn stash."

There's a pause, punctuated only by her deep breathing.

"What now?" I ask. This seems to break her reverie.

"Bus station is the only thing that makes sense. We'll catch him there." She leans down, arm reaching below the seat. Moments later, there's a snubnosed revolver in her hand. She puts this in her purse.

"Hello," I cough out. "You keep a spare, or what?"

Morgan says nothing, only starts the car. She reaches out to close her door as she backs up; the tires give a little yelp as her foot hits the floor.

"How do you know where Jack is?"

China hands flex on the wheel. "He's only got cash. He doesn't have a picture ID, so he can't fly. He'll want to get as far away from me as he can, and that means the bus station. There's a Greyhound a few miles from the hospital."

We twist through the streets, behind shopping centers and warehouses. Some small creature rests atop a trash bin—cat, possum or raccoon—but runs scurrying as we rush past.

Within minutes, we're parking in the lot of a Greyhound bus station. The digital display on the dash says 4:23 AM, but even still, bodies litter the exterior of the building. Most sprawl out across the cement like casualties after a battle, with heads on backpacks and faces covered by jackets. At the far corner of the building, a set of eyes gleam behind a stream of cigarette smoke.

"You're going to have to help me," Morgan says. "Go check in the lobby; I'm going to circle the building. If you see him, just come find me." She puts the purse's strap over her shoulder. "Come on."

I blink twice. A dull ache returns to my leg; the morphine is fading fast, and I feel strangely hollow. My blood chafes through raw veins.

I sit at the edge of the car seat and face the concrete. One crutch gains a grip on the parking lot, then the other. I wobble upright, catching myself on their aluminum legs. Fighting back nausea, I take a step with my good leg, then catch myself with the crutches.

The pain in my knee is fresh, cleaner and brighter than before, from new incisions. However, the cast is a marvel, and puts the weight of my mangled leg on my hip. The black plastic holds me in a slightly crooked position, and the leg hangs a few inches from the ground when I'm standing.

Morgan is already behind the building by the time I hobble to the bus station's front office. I struggle to pull open the heavy Plexiglas door, getting one crutch inside to prop it open, then climbing the rest of the way through. The sweat that coats me is cold on clammy skin.

The bus station is mostly deserted. Two flat screen televisions are mounted over the front desk, where an older black man in a Greyhound shirt reads a magazine. Aside from him, I'm alone.

Relieved, I push my way outside, searching for Morgan. My palms are sweaty on the gray foam grips of the crutches. The click, stomp, clack of my shambling tripod momentum takes me around the bus station, past a woman in green flannel and her kid.

I circle the building: there's no sign of Morgan or Jack.

Then I hear a faint sound, at the edges of my perception. A warble, something that doesn't fit.

It's coming from inside. I didn't see anyone in the lobby, though, and—the restrooms. They open from outside; the men's room is around the corner. I shuffle the few feet to the bathroom entrance and push my way inside, entering sideways and using my body to wedge open the door.

Morgan's back is turned, and I follow the crook in her elbow to the revolver she holds. The trajectory of the barrel leads across the bathroom to Jack, who stands with his hands in the air. A black duffel bag rests at his feet.

"Shoot him," I say. "Do us all a favor."

As though clockwork, all eyes flit to me for a moment, then resume their positions.

"You can't keep me under your thumb like this," Jack says, addressing Morgan. "I can't be a hostage. You and Banks are making a mockery of the whole ghost concept. You've got more money, you've got a new pet, just let me go."

"Jack, you know what I can do to you, don't you?" Morgan asks. "Is that what you want?"

"It's probably in this bag right now," Jack counters. "One more reason not to give it to you."

"Would you rather be shot?" she asks. "Weigh your options."

"Get it over with, then," Jack says, voice louder. "Shoot me, or put me in prison, just stop holding me prisoner."

Morgan grunts, then turns to me. "Hold this," she says. "The safety is off. Pull the trigger if he tries anything."

And she hands me the gun—I've never held one. It's cold, and much heavier than I thought. I rest my wrist across the top of the crutch, so the little metal cross at the tip of the barrel lines up with Jack's chest. I keep my finger off the trigger, because that feels electric when I touch it, almost burns my finger.

Morgan walks the five feet across the bathroom tile to Jack, then bends down to pick up the duffel bag.

When she bends down, Jack squats, grabbing the bag with both hands and ramming into Morgan with his shoulders—she falls to the floor. Jack charges me, bag of money clutched to his chest.

The moment he begins the motion, my hand clenches reflexively, but my finger hits the guard and not the trigger. I reposition, squeeze again; still nothing—it takes more force. I squeeze harder, and there's a tremendous *pop*.

He's only a foot away by the time I manage to fire. It's so loud I can practically see the sound; my vision goes white. Morgan shrieks as Jack spins, groaning and dropping the bag.

A white tile spritzed with a mist of Jack's blood falls from the bathroom wall and shatters on the floor.

"Are you fucking kidding me?" Jack bellows, left arm grabbing his right, twisting violently. He lets out a long hiss, some pressurized tank ruptured.

The gun trembles in my grip. Morgan kicks the bag behind me; it slides across the tile floor. Her arm extends, followed by the hot breath of her sigh, then her hand is resting on top of the revolver. The whole move is tired, but diplomatic. "It's okay, Sean," she whispers. It barely registers through the ringing in my ears. "Sean, it's okay. Give me the gun."

My fingers don't want to come unclenched. Her left hand joins her right, warmth of them circling the weapon, melting my resistance. Morgan tugs; I relent, liquefied. The gunmetal sticks to my skin as she draws it away.

"Listen to me," she says, voice calm. "We need to get out of here right now. Someone probably heard that, and the police are probably on their way. Just follow me."

Jack growls low, voice hysterical as his rumbling moan of pain tangles itself into a tight whimper. With his left arm, he pulls the jacket from his right side. Blood spills down to the tiles, drooling from the open mouth of his sleeve, splattered behind him as it swings to the side.

He looks into the bathroom mirror; we watch his arm, transfixed. The wound appears small, only a bloody hole the size of a pencil eraser clean through his right bicep.

I shot him, I realize.

And just two weeks ago, I was such a good kid.

"Come on, everyone, let's go," Morgan calls. Always composed. Always, all ways.

Jack pulls the jacket back up over his wound. With the dark material covering him, it's not easy to tell he's been shot. I notice he bundles the end of the sleeve where his hand should come out, to keep the blood trapped inside.

And then all three of us are leaving the bathroom like nothing happened. Jack is rigid, face paling as he struggles to control himself. I hobble behind him, crutches suddenly heavier, as the shock leaves me weak. Morgan leads.

The bodies strewn across the bus station stare up at us with gleaming eyes, animals lying in cover. They've multiplied in number; our ruckus attracted attention.

When we get to the car, she hands me the duffel bag. I toss it in, then stretch out across the back seat. Jack curses and moans his way into the front.

"I can't believe you shot me," he mutters darkly.

I can't either, honestly. I do hate this man, but, damn. Still, Sean Reilly is dead—who's to say what the new me can and can't do?

22. To scrape

THE CAR IS MORE TRIAGE UNIT than vehicle; Jack presses a palm to the bloody hole in his arm and I brace against his seat to keep my broken knee from rolling around the cabin.

"This is all going fantastically," I announce. "And my morphine wore off."

"Shut up, Sean," Morgan says, voice cold. "We're being followed."

I twist in the seat. A pair of headlights illuminate the night behind us, distorted into burning suns by the dust coating the Cadillac's rear window. As we pass another street light, I get a glimpse of the car's full profile: a rack of lights are mounted on the hood.

"It's a cop," I say.

"Hide the bag. Look normal, Jack."

"Nothing to it," he groans, pulling a blood-covered hand from the inside of his jacket. He fumbles with the zipper, closing his coat.

I push the duffel bag under my seat, aware that a single glance inside will get us all sent straight to jail.

Emergency lights engage, and the damp peace of a Louisiana night is bombarded by flashes of blue and white. Morgan pulls to a stop between street lights, so the car sits in an hourglass figure of darkness.

"Everyone calm, be normal." She fixes her hair in the rear view mirror. "If you're not nervous, he won't be nervous."

I settle into my seat. So this is it, then. I'm going to end up in prison after all. Oh well—I gave it my best shot.

"Calm," Morgan repeats, glancing back at me. "No suspicion, no search. We just picked you up from the bus station; you left from Los Angeles, where your family lives. You're Ryan White."

"The ID is in the bag," Jack says through grit teeth.

I both hear and feel the faint thud of the officer's car door slamming shut. I'm staring straight ahead, so the first evidence of his presence comes from his flashlight's beam shining on the back of Morgan's seat.

She rolls down the window. His searching light is focused on her face, then Jack's, then into the backseat and at me. I squint into the glow. Still can't see him; he's just a spotlight and a silhouette.

"License and registration, please," the officer says as the beam snaps back to Morgan.

Morgan presents a folded slip of paper. His hand glows red in the focused light as he reaches out and takes it.

"Can I ask where you're headed this late at night?" the officer asks, searing each of our retinas in turn with his light.

"Picking up our friend from the bus station," Morgan says politely, pointing a thumb over her shoulder.

I wave meekly to the officer.

"Where do you live?" he asks, pointing his flashlight at the papers in his hand, reading Morgan's insurance and driver's license.

"I'm from Florida," Morgan says. "Orlando."

"I live in New Orleans," Jack offers. "They're all here to connect with me." His voice sounds tight, strained. Small wonder, with the bullet wound in his arm.

"And who are you?" the policeman asks him.

Good question.

"I'm Hank," Jack says. Though he's managed to force a grin, it's clear to me that he's struggling. The sheen of sweat across his forehead reflects the flashlight, and he talks with a clenched jaw. His complexion is faintly green.

"Let me ask," the officer says, tapping Morgan's documents against the back of the hand which holds the light. "Did any of ya'll see or hear anything strange at the Greyhound station?"

Jack speaks immediately, eyes wide: "Yeah! There was a loud popping sound—remember that?" he asks. Morgan and I nod in agreement. "We figured a car backfired, you know?"

"Around what time?" the officer asks.

"About twenty minutes ago? Wait, wait. Was that a gunshot?" Jack turns to Morgan. "You don't think...that guy we saw?"

Morgan nods excitedly. "That creepy guy," she says. "With the duffel bag, in the men's bathroom? You think he shot someone in there?"

Jack turns back to the cop, talking fast. "Dude. I was in the bathroom, this guy comes in. White guy, dressed in black, duffel bag. I left as soon as I saw him, he looked scary as shit."

Morgan jumps in: "I saw him walk up to the bus station and go straight into the bathroom. Didn't stop to get a ticket or anything."

Jack picks up where she left off: "You think he killed someone? Damn, that could have been me. Jesus, look, I've got goose bumps."

"What about you? Hear anything?" he shines the light in my eyes.

I don't want to talk. Instead, I just nod in agreement.

"He's a little shy," Morgan supplies.

The cop shakes his head, motions for me to roll down the window. I do so, though it is childproof and only opens halfway.

"What's your name?" he asks.

I swallow, try to talk as American as possible. "Ryan White," I say.

"You seem a little young to be traveling across the country by bus. Let me see some identification."

Jack pipes in: "Sir, that man is probably still at the bus station. He could have murdered someone!"

"Quiet," the officer says, voice sharp. Then he turns to me. "ID, please."

I nod. It's in the duffel bag—the bag filled with money and a handgun. I make a big show of adjusting my broken knee, moving it to the other side of the floorboard, then pretending to struggle as I reach for the bag. My new position allows me to keep the contents out of sight. When I reach inside, I unzip it only enough to fit my hand in, then begin feeling around.

I feel the cash, and the pistol—then, finally, the little plastic booklet with Ryan White's social security card, birth certificate and credit card. I pull out the social security card, then push the bag closed.

He takes the little blue card, shines a light on it, and looks skeptical.

"You don't have a driver's license?" he asks.

I shake my head 'no.'

"And where are you from?"

"California," I say, speaking slowly.

The policeman grips the radio on his chest, brings it up to his mouth. "Can I get a check on a social security number?"

It chirps something back, unintelligible. He reads the number aloud.

A tense minute later, the radio squawks back: "Ryan White, nineteen, brown hair, Caucasian male."

He returns the card to me, then steps to the driver's side window, pointing his flashlight at Jack.

"What do you do for a living, Hank?" he asks.

Now that I'm re-positioned directly behind him, I can't see Jack's face. On his right side, though, I see something even worse—the door panel below his wound is soaked in blood, thick and dark like cherry syrup. It drips from the seat belt.

"Welder, usually. Right now, I collect unemployment," Jack says, then grins. The sweat is visible on his forehead.

"Is something wrong?" the officer asks.

A whimper escapes Jack's throat; he swallows hard. "Just thinking about that shooter," he says. "Could be a massacre over there." A drop of blood falls from his coat, and I hear it land with a soft tap.

The officer shakes his head. He seems to struggle, face tight, hand on his chin. After a long pause, he speaks: "I have your license plate and IDs recorded. I find out you're bullshitting me, I'm going to come find you." He pounds on the top of the car. "Get rolling."

Morgan rolls up the windows and turns the key. "He'll create a record of this," she says. The car revs to life; she pulls slowly into traffic. "We can't go back to the hotel. We've got to keep moving, we've got to change states, get a new car."

The thought of hours in the car with Jack brings a wave of depression. I was in surgery a few hours ago; the pain is coming in increasing waves, a tide rising. I lean back and stare up at the roof of the car, hoping somehow I'll be able to sleep.

23. Escape artists

WE STOP ONCE, at a gas station an hour from Lake Charles. While I pump gas, Morgan returns from the store carrying a plastic bag filled with gauze, paper towels, duct tape, rubbing alcohol, and various other supplies hidden from view.

"That's disgusting," Morgan says, nodding at the interior of the car near Jack's wound. Blood thickened over the material, leaving a burgundy crust on the fabric around him.

"Oh jeez, I'm sorry," Jack mumbles. "Did a little bit of my dying get on your car?"

"You're not dying," Morgan tells him. "He barely shot you."

The morphine is gone from my system, and as we exit the gas station, an uneasiness settles over me.

Jack struggles to pull the jacket from his wound—the inner lining is stuck against his skin, and he hisses when it peels away. The pile of makeshift medical supplies sit in his lap, only reflected by the occasional streetlamp shining overhead. They pulse intermittently, each yellow bulb crossing the car like a sun rising and falling. The thousand days of our night.

"Is it always like this?" I ask.

"Like what?" Jack asks, jaw clenched in pain.

"I don't know," I say. "Frantic. Running, hiding. Police showing up at random."

"Things are usually a lot calmer," Morgan informs. "It's been months since I dealt with the police. This whole situation is a mess, and you are toxic. Don't take that the wrong way, it's entirely Jack's fault. But for now, you should expect it. You talked about faking a death before you disappeared. We didn't leave them a body. You're being hunted, at least for now. When enough time passes, things will go back to normal. But, when the police do come, it's always like that. You blink, and you're one second from prison. They try to catch you off guard. Never blink, always be ready."

"Firing a gun in a public bathroom doesn't help," Jack says. "People seem to notice that, complain. And all those people at the bus station start remembering things."

"You forced his hand," Morgan corrects.

"I didn't think he would be that stupid. Losing the money is the rational option."

"I'm not feeling very rational," I say. "I'm feeling the opposite of rational, in fact."

"I think you're doing very well," Morgan reassures me. "I'm glad you shot Jack." She looks at him. "Sorry, but you shouldn't try to steal from me. I'm helping you."

"You're blackmailing me," he says. Then, after a pause, his voice softens. "And helping me. Your apprentice here is just homesick."

My first reaction is to reject his accusation. But—I am, I realize. There is a sick pit in my stomach, and as it burns, it reminds me that nothing—absolutely nothing—will ever be the same again. My old life is gone, and there is no going back.

A road stretches out before us, long and flat, fed to us in thirty yard portions illuminated by the car's headlamps. The path runs east, to Mississippi. In the space where the asphalt meets the night sky, a deep violet promises the coming dawn.

Jack hisses as he presses an alcohol-soaked paper towel to his arm. He brushes the purple wound roughly with a wad, scraping away dried blood. "You're learning to live without a shadow."

"I swear to God, if you start talking about shadows, I will shoot you again."

Jack clucks his tongue. "Only because you don't understand."

"You're right, Jack, I don't understand. No one could understand, because you're a crazy person."

He pours more alcohol on the wound, then rubs it again with paper towels. The red gore softens to pink as it comes clean.

"Your shadow is your shared persona. It's the part of you that everyone knows, but it's not you, not exactly. Your reputation, your public identity. It's the only thing we ever know of another person. Your shadow is the thing inside everyone else that died when they found out Sean Reilly was gone. Everyone has a shadow, and when it's dark, they're all together—creating this social network that governs us, that shapes our existence."

"Jack once embarked on a project to try just about every psychedelic drug on Earth, several times," Morgan says. "Don't think too hard about what he says."

"Don't make excuses for me," Jack says. "I know exactly what I'm saying."

"Stop talking. You killed Kayla," I tell him, voice flat. Just saying this makes me angry. Hate listening to him talk like he has something to teach me. She was a good person, and he butchered her.

Jack covers his thin bicep in gauze, which quickly turns pink, then bites the end of the cotton material to pull the wrapping tight.

"Kayla didn't know the value of a dollar," he says.

Morgan interjects: "You're free, aren't you? We escaped."

"Is that supposed to make me feel better?" I ask. "At least Jack's framing me didn't result in my going to prison forever? Some prize. If that bullet hit Jack about a foot to the left, that would make me feel better."

"That'll make you a murderer," he says quietly. "You don't like murder, remember?"

"Everyone who would miss you already thinks you're dead. I'd just be making it true," I answer.

A strip of duct tape is stretched; Jack wraps it around his arm, then tears it. He doesn't respond—this makes me even angrier.

"Why are we putting up with his shit, Morgan?" I ask. "Can't we stop the car, drop him off? He tried to steal from you; hell, Kayla's not even the first person he's murdered. Jack killed Cole's wife, too."

Jack barks out a short, hollow laugh. "You hear that?" he asks Morgan. "He thinks you two are a 'we.'" He turns to me. "You have no idea what you're talking about. Is that some big reveal you saved up? *Cole?* Fucking Cole Durham? That piece of shit is still sneaking around?"

"Shut up, Jack," Morgan says quietly.

"Cole came to me and told me you killed his wife," I answer, body like stone, face forward. "And I would have told him how to find you, if I knew. You're a psychopath and you need to be in prison."

"That's rich!" he exclaims.

"Jack," Morgan warns, but he speaks over her.

"You think I killed Cole's wife? She's driving this car, you idiot. Listen carefully: *Morgan is Cole's wife.*"

"Shut the hell up, Jack," Morgan repeats, except this time her voice is barely a whisper.

24. Smoke

I DON'T KNOW WHAT TO SAY, and so say nothing. The car falls to uneasy silence.

Cole and Morgan. I think back to his strange desperation, the way he jumped all over any mention of a girl traveling with Jack. It made sense.

Does he know she's alive? Why did she run away?

I even thought of calling him again, after I jumped, just to tell him where to find Jack. I couldn't risk giving up my secret, though, not to a sheriff. Now, I'm glad I didn't. He must be after Morgan as much as Jack.

These thoughts keep me occupied as the sun rises around us, and morning burns its path down the road toward our car. Sunlight wakes the swampland; deer graze in the morning light, chewing cautiously on greens at the edge of the tree line.

After an hour down a narrow farm road, Morgan speaks: "Is this the turn?"

Jack turns around and puts a hand on the black duffel bag, which he pulls into the front seat as I stare nervously. He unzips the bag and fetches a slim, rectangular smartphone. Once it's turned on, he reports: "Yeah, turn here."

I lean up and take the bag back, once he's finished.

We turn off the highway and on a gravel road; rocks are kicked up by the car and bounce noisily off the undercarriage. Tall ferns and moss-devoured trees line the road and wall us in—the vegetation here is aggressive, claiming everything.

"Stop here," Jack says. "It's a half-mile up."

The car slows, then reverses. Morgan maneuvers to a small trail, almost invisible from the road—just two tracks of sand half grown-over with weeds. The path winds through the trees for maybe a hundred yards, until we reach a clearing.

The rusted-out shell of an old Volvo, half a trailer, and a few rotting logs are piled atop a base of roof shingles and plastic panels of various sizes. Trash bags lay slain, torn apart and spilling their innards. We've arrived at someone's private dump.

We park in two feet of weeds. Locusts scatter, some flying kamikaze into the side of the car as Jack and Morgan open their doors.

"What's up?" I ask, cracking my own door open and pulling myself halfway out. I push my crutches into the earth; they shift uneasily, sliding as plants crack and snap beneath them.

Morgan opens the door opposite mine and retrieves the duffel bag. "We need a new car," she says as she rests the bag on the hood and withdraws a stack of cash. "This one has Jack all over it, and a cop saw us." She flips through the money and pinches off about a quarter of one stack—dozens of hundred dollar bills.

"Come here," Morgan says to Jack.

"You want me to go get it?" he asks.

"Yeah. Here." The bundle of bills shake in her hand. "Be quick."

He takes the money, nods, and sets off back the direction from which we came. In moments, he is out of sight.

"You trust him with that?"

"That's twenty grand. He wants to run away for twenty grand, he's more than welcome." As she speaks, she walks over to the driver's seat. The bag of gas station supplies lays open; she reaches in and grabs a pack of cigarettes and several books of matches.

Morgan smacks the pack of cigarettes on the underside of her wrist four times, then rips the cellophane off and pulls out a cigarette. "I'm going to teach you a trick. You'll need tricks, if you want to survive."

Her lipstick is cracked and faded, some sun-worn graffiti, all upscale vandal. The cigarette is placed between her lips; she lights it and inhales deeply, holding it in for several seconds. Savoring it. Moments later, smoke streams from her mouth.

"Didn't know you smoked," I say.

"Only when I have to. How are you doing?" she asks, arms folded across the loosely knit sweater that drapes her upper body.

"I'm...I don't even know. Lonely. I keep wanting to reach for my phone, to text someone. I miss the Internet, I miss my friends, my parents. It's hard to describe. I feel, I don't know. Empty."

"I meant your leg," Morgan says, grinning.

I laugh. "That hurts, too."

Her pale shoulders are slumped, sloping downward into arms crossed under her chest, one hand tilted up with the cigarette. The expression on her face is vacant, natural; she stares into the trash pit as she speaks.

"It's a process," she tells me. "Just keep calm, it's only hard at first. You think you lost yourself, but you're just starting to realize what you are in the first place. Not Sean, but something underneath it. The thing which drove Sean." She takes a long drag of the cigarette. "You want to know why I'm running from Cole?"

"Only if you want to tell me," I say. "I'm running from every cop in the world, I don't need to hear each individual reason why."

Morgan smiles as she takes another drag. "I like you. You're smart. I wouldn't take you in, otherwise. You wouldn't survive this long." She pushes a strand of hair behind her ear.

"It's only been a few days. Give me some time, I'll get killed."

She smiles again. "I got married at seventeen. Dropped out of school, got my GED. Things went okay with Cole at first. He was always an angry guy, but never at me. I used to like it, in a way, when he got all fired up—usually to defend me from one thing or another, real or otherwise."

She pulls another cigarette from the pack and holds it between the index and middle fingers of her left hand, which she extends toward me. "Take it," she says. "Hold it in your mouth."

I do so.

Morgan approaches, stepping toward me, coming uncomfortably close. Soon, we're less than a foot apart.

"What are you—" I start to ask, lips bending around the cigarette.

Instead of answering, she leans in, face coming toward mine, eyes closed. Soon I can feel the heat from her cigarette, can smell the smoke on her breath.

Our cigarettes touch—hers smoldering, mine unlit.

"Inhale," she says from between clenched lips, face inches away.

I do so. The ember climbs from hers to mine, and acrid smoke coats my tongue. It tastes terrible; I pull it from my mouth and hold the burning stick between two fingers.

Still, my pulse is racing.

Morgan takes a step back, then pulls another cigarette from the pack, hands it to me.

"I don't want to smoke these," I say.

"Don't smoke them. Just light them, we're going to use them for something."

I do as she says, putting the fresh cigarette between my lips, pressing the lit one to it, then inhaling. This time I don't pull too hard, and the smoke doesn't get in my lungs.

"We were together for years, and Cole's life became a series of disappointments. He failed the State Trooper's exam, wound up at some little sheriff's office. We were always broke. Cole needed to be angry with someone, but everyone else was sick of him at that point. Someone needed to be blamed, and I was the only one who hadn't left him. That's when he started beating me."

"I'm sorry," I murmur, but Morgan brushes this out of the air with her hand, the motion trailed by a stream of gray smoke.

"He used to beat the shit out of me, pretty often. He's a cop, too, and I know how it is. They protect each other, try to keep each other out of the news. Cole would threaten me, say he'd kill me if I told anyone. And after several years of being terrified for my life every day, I met Jack."

Morgan takes what remains of her cigarette and presses it between the paper folds of the matchbook, then closes the book around it.

"Jack offered me a way out. He was freedom. He was working with Mr. Banks to scam this insurance company where Banks is an executive. Jack did the legwork and Banks kept anyone from asking questions. Jack told me he needed help, offered to take me in, to make me disappear. I figured Cole would kill me eventually, so I guess it didn't seem so insane. I went from abused wife to proud owner of a million dollar duffel bag."

Morgan steps up to the car and places the bundled cigarette and book of matches under the seat. Smoke streams up from the beige leather as the cigarette burns itself, inching toward the point when ember will meet matchbook.

"And something else happened," she says. "The person I used to be—the frightened, abused woman who at times even blamed herself for everything, that person dropped away. First, I felt lost and depressed. I kept trying to recreate myself, to find my place in the world. Until one day, I stopped trying. I just let myself be empty, and not have a place. And that's when things got better. That's what Jack means about losing your shadow. Losing that link to the world of people, to the community."

"And Cole is still following you?" I ask. "He doesn't think you're dead?" There are now three lit cigarettes in my hand; she takes one and puts it between a second matchbook.

"I know he's still following me. I don't know what else he knows; I've never spoken with him. If he catches me, I don't know what he'll do. Kill me, maybe." Morgan puts this one on the other side of the car, under the seat. "He believes I belong to him. To slip my leash was the ultimate insult."

I hand her another cigarette; this goes between a third book of matches, and is tucked away underneath the trunk, with the spare tire.

Morgan takes the last cigarette from my hand, but only places it between her lips. The tip glows as she inhales.

"Normally, we get away from the car now. The whole point of the matchbook trick is giving yourself time to get away before everyone starts freaking out over the fire. But today, I feel like watching something burn."

A demonic hiss comes from the car's front seat; the first cigarette burns down until the little coal touches the cardboard box. The fire climbs, lighting match tips in a blaze of phosphor, setting off a chain reaction until a four-inch pile of red flame licks the underside of the car seat.

The other two matchbooks are quick to follow, and black smoke streams from the open doors, heralding the arrival of flame which soon consumes the front seats and reaches the roof of the car.

"Not bad," I say as foam bubbles and melts, as plastic cracks and warps under the heat. I take a few steps to the right, next to Morgan, so that I'm clear from the acrid smoke. She takes another drag from her cigarette, eyes fixed on the fire.

Minutes later, a horn honks, breaking my trance.

"That'll be Jack," she says.

25. This time, no drowning

THE NEW CAR IS AN UPGRADE, a silver Mercedes with leather seats that heat at the press of a button. The engine rumbles low when Morgan pushes the pedal, igniting into a roar as she accelerates up a ramp and onto an interstate.

"I take it you didn't leave me any change?" she asks Jack, who only shrugs.

"We'll get there twice as fast, now," he notes. "V8."

We drive away the morning, crossing through Mobile, Alabama into Florida, hugging the southern coast.

Morgan makes one stop, at Jack's insistence, at a decrepit RV in a trailer park a few miles into Florida. This is preceded by a brief phone conversation in which he orders something conspicuous, and ends with Jack returning to the car with a dirty grocery bag.

The plastic rustles as he digs inside. A brown plastic bottle, the kind you find hydrogen peroxide in at the store, comes up in his hand. In place of a label are streaks of papered glue, where it's been rubbed away.

"Ether," Jack explains. "For the pain."

I speak: "What century is this? Get some Vicodin."

"Trust me, this is better. Want some?" The cap is off; he extends the flask to me. I wave it away.

"Crack a goddamn window," Morgan orders.

Jack does so, then holds the bottle a few inches under his nose. He whimpers softly and leans back in his seat.

Anything to shut him up.

It isn't until we're thirty miles from Ocala, Florida that Morgan speaks: "Do you have the address?"

"Exit here," Jack says, voice slurred. "Second light, take a right."

"You sure, druggy?" Morgan asks.

"I got shot, goddamnit. You wrap up a gunshot wound with duct tape, then tell me how you feel."

Palm trees line the feeder road like Seussian invaders, entirely out of place in a landscape devoured by weeds and moss. Vines overtake a faded brown picket fence. Beyond that, an elderly horse with a sloping spine chews on the grass at his feet.

Jack directs us to a suburban neighborhood with stately homes on large plots of land, big yards with stone walls. We creep through the streets as Morgan cranes her neck to check black addresses painted on curbs. After some searching, she pulls into the driveway of a two-story gray brick house—a chimney climbs from the roof, and smoke escapes, despite the fact it's a hot day.

"This is home," Morgan answers as she parks the car and opens her door. I follow, struggling with my crutches.

"Seriously?" I ask. "This is amazing."

Georgian columns frame the front door, and I lean against the left, smelling the fresh paint on its softly angled edges.

Jack lifts the mat and finds a key. He steps inside, letting the door slam on Morgan—she opens it again, then holds it for me as I hobble through.

The house is frigid; someone left the air conditioner running full blast. This, along with granite floors and broad windows streaming light, contributes to the crisp, modern feel of the home. The living room's vaulted ceiling is supported by wooden beams, and is less decorated than designed. Nooks and borders cut across the otherwise bare walls and ceiling, carving angles out of the space.

"Holy hell," Jack murmurs. He is ahead of us, and blocks my view of the living room.

"What?" Morgan asks, then falls silent.

I scuttle in from behind. A fire burns across the foyer of the house, and someone sits in the recliner, facing the flames. A square glass of amber liquid rests in his hand.

Mr. Banks rotates in the leather recliner until he faces us; the chair rocks softly when he stops.

"Glad you could make it," he says. "More or less in one piece." Then he squints at Jack's arm, my leg. "Maybe less."

"Good to see you," Morgan says, standing straight, voice calm. She walks stiffly to the kitchen and puts her purse on the counter, then turns to watch Jack.

He stands, red-faced, stuttering out a sentence that never fully forms.

At the far end of the living room sits a sofa, a good twenty feet from Mr. Banks. I decide to sit here, and rest my crutches against the couch cushions. Given Jack's reaction, it seems they have something to work out.

Jack finally finds himself. "I didn't think I'd see you again," he says, taking the seat next to Mr. Banks. He faces the floor, lips pressed together, and scratches at the top of his makeshift bandage.

"I have a deal you're going to take," Mr. Banks says, addressing Jack.

"Oh yeah?"

"I need you to kill yourself. Again."

"It's too soon," Jack says immediately. "Police just stopped us yesterday. Let things relax a little bit. A month."

"We can't," Mr. Banks says. "You two fucked everything up."

I see Morgan rock back on her feet as a pained expression glances across her face.

He continues: "I have people who expected Kayla's insurance to pay out, who were counting on that money. I need to keep them friendly, and that means you two are going to fix your mistake, and you're not going to get paid for doing it."

Jack clutches the back of his own neck. "Who's gonna die?"

"A wealthy widower, Ronald Silver. Recently sold his foreign assets and bought an RV. He's insured for two million dollars, payable to his daughter."

"You want me to run around breaking laws when I know the police are looking? For free?"

Mr. Banks folds one leg over the other and takes a sip from his glass. "I am not a complete asshole. If you do this, I will give you a new identity. You can run off on your own, then, and be free of us."

"Is there any more of that?" Jack points at the glass in the older man's hand.

"Morgan, would you be a dear?" he asks. "Pour yourself one as well. And Sean, too."

I hear ice clinking against glass, then the rhythmic *chug* of pouring. Morgan exits the kitchen with two half-filled glasses; one goes to me, and the other to Jack.

Mr. Banks speaks: "As I said, you won't be paid. But, Sean will. Show him how you do it, before I set you free."

Jack dumps the scotch down his throat. He holds the glass out, and Morgan refills it.

"You expect me to do what, exactly?" I ask. "Kill people?" The question flies from my mouth before I can reign it in.

Jack answers: "See? He doesn't know shit. He's a kid, seriously. You think he's going to replace me?"

Mr. Banks grins slightly as he speaks: "No, Morgan is going to replace you. Sean is going to collect for her."

"Why me?" I ask.

"Because you'll never betray me," he answers. "Because the police will never believe what you have to say, if you try. You need us." Another sip. "But mostly, because Morgan said she'd do it."

"He'll pay you," Morgan adds. "A lot. You need money, or you won't survive. You are wanted for murder. If you can't find a place to sleep at night, if you can't travel, then you're going to prison for the rest of your life."

I don't know what to say.

"So, it's settled," Mr. Banks says.

"I didn't agree," Jack interjects, standing.

"You don't need to," he answers. "We both know what you're going to do. Oh, and one more thing—this policy doesn't cover drowning. You'll need to expand the playbook." Mr. Banks sets his glass on the table, then rises and begins walking across the stone floor.

Jack swears, turns and hurls his empty glass into the fire. It strikes the wall of the fireplace and explodes; small shards rocket outward, orange in the light of the fire. These clink as they land on the granite floor.

I turn to look out the window; a black luxury sedan is parked on the street. As our benefactor leaves the house and walks down the driveway, a man in a tuxedo and black cap gets out the driver's side and opens the passenger door. When Mr. Banks is seated within, he drives off.

26. What I haven't done

WE SIT AROUND THE LAST EMBERS of Mr. Banks' fire, in leather recliners that smell like a new wallet. Morgan drank several more glasses of scotch, and I didn't. Jack left in a fury, hours ago.

"I don't get it," I say. "What am I expected to do?"

Morgan takes a sip from her glass. "When you get life insurance, a company pays money to your wife or kids in case you die—so they don't starve without you. I'm going to pretend to be Ronald Silver's daughter, and collect after Jack makes it look like he died. Assuming we survive, later on, you'll pretend to be the son of whoever I pretend to kill next."

"I get that," I say. "But who is Ronald Silver in the first place? Don't people get suspicious when someone who looks like Jack pretends to kill himself over and over again?"

"Saying we kill *ourselves* is not really accurate. I killed myself, like you, to start a new life. Once, to emancipate myself. But our scam, our art, is to create a fake life, and then end that one. Ronald Silver never existed, and never will. Let me ask you—if you found a boat, belonging to a man, upturned on a beach somewhere—wouldn't you wonder if the boat's owner was missing? And then his children, who perhaps look an awful lot like Jack and I, insist the boat's owner took the boat out just two days ago. And we take you to his home, filled with trinkets and photographs of a man no one has ever seen in person, but who seems to be completely real. We convince the authorities—after we lay down some bribes to keep anyone looking too hard—that someone who never lived, has died. This is our craft, and you'll be learning it."

"And the thing about not drowning?"

"Drowning is the easiest way to do it. There's always the problem of coming up with a body, so it's best to create a situation where the body may not be found."

"And what will it take to make Ronald Silver seem real?"

"Surprisingly little. Now, let's celebrate," Morgan tells me.

"What are we celebrating?"

"New house, new city. Have you seen the backyard?"

I shake my head 'no.'

"Come on, then," Morgan says, rising from the recliner, glass of scotch in one hand. I follow her across the kitchen, where she snatches the bottle of liquor. We exit through a wooden door paneled with frosted glass, and are met by a warm Florida night.

The backyard seems like the sort of painting Mrs. McPherson would pick lovingly out of a garage sale while Kayla and I gagged from out of eyesight. Too cliché, too Americana. A wooden gazebo perches on a green mound, and behind that, a white picket fence. A small red shed made to look like the classic American barn fills one corner.

In front of all this lays a swimming pool that glows neon blue against the dark of the evening. Underwater lights give it an unearthly aura, radiance made to bend and dance in the fluid.

Morgan takes a seat on a nearby deck chair, inches from the edge of the water, and slips off her black flats. Pale feet extend from blue jeans and reflect the liquid light, toenails flawless, painted a wet, deep red.

I sit in the chair next to her, reclining back and staring up at a starless night sky. I don't know what to say, and so say nothing.

"Don't be a buzzkill," she complains after a moment.

"What did I say?"

"You didn't say anything. You never say anything." There's another pause, where I continue to 'never say anything.' Morgan continues: "How about we go out, tomorrow? Do whatever you want, whatever you can think up. I'll pay for it all."

"Thanks," I murmur.

She's being nice again. Makes me uncomfortable.

"What's the problem?" Morgan presses.

"I know that you're manipulating me. All the time, really. When we first met, when you were hugging me after bailing me out, being so nice, that's just what you were doing, right? Being nice, because being nice is what would get the job done fastest. Being nice is what would keep me from running to the police and making everything difficult."

"And putting yourself in prison," she adds.

"Yeah, and that. I mean, let's assume it was for my own good. So you're like this benevolent puppet master. But—you're too good at it. How do I know when you're manipulating, and when you're the real...whatever you are?"

Morgan sighs heavily, chest thrusting skyward then deflating slowly. I don't want to watch, but can't help it.

She speaks: "All the petty stuff people fight for, they do it because they are still their names. Sean wants credit for something he did, because he wants to build the Sean brand. Or Sean can't let his feelings get hurt, because then it damages the Sean name. When you lose a name, you stop worrying about all that. There is no brand I'm trying to build; I switch to whatever I want. I don't feel there is any Morgan I need to defend, so I am free to act effectively."

"You must be able to set it all aside, though. You must have some real friends in the world, right? People you can relax around?"

Morgan does not answer. Instead, we sit in silence. I take that silence, and out of the immutable blankness, draw the only conclusion to be drawn.

"What do you want to do tomorrow?" she asks. Her voice is perky, friendly even.

"I want to be a person again."

"You're a person, now. More of a person than you have ever been, Sean. Now tell me, what do you want to do?"

"Admitting that I know you're only manipulating me again, to appease me—I guess I don't really know what I want to do."

Morgan leans up, turns to face me, and rests on one arm. "I tell you that you can do anything you want, regardless of expense, and you don't know what you want to do? Where's your imagination?"

"I guess I don't know what I want anymore," I answer. "We've just been running. Everything is so—I don't know. I'm a fugitive, you know? I guess I'm still figuring out what this life is."

We're silent for a moment, and I listen to crickets chirp from an oak tree that rises over the yard.

I turn to face Morgan, to watch her face, but realize her new position places her cleavage directly in my line of sight; I glance, then look her in the eyes. The same blue satellites. This also proves too intense, and so I direct my eyes at the unearthly glow of the swimming pool.

"Let's flip that on its head. What haven't you done?" Her voice is soft, halfway to a whisper.

"Almost everything," I say, realizing it's true.

"Narrow that down a little," she says, taking a sip from her drink. Her breasts shift as her hand rises to her mouth.

"Oh, I don't know. I've never given it much thought." All the usual bucket list clichés spring to mind. "I've never seen the Grand Canyon, or Paris, or the pyramids. I've never swam with dolphins, or jumped out of an airplane, or bungee jumped."

"Though you did jump off a very tall bridge," she notes.

"Good point. I've never even seen a good mountain before, the kind I see in pictures. I want to feel tiny. When you put it that way, when you ask me what I haven't done, I guess the answer is 'a whole lot.' Hell, I've never been drunk."

"Don't have to wait for that," she informs, then lifts the scotch from its position on the ground between us. I take it, and lay the bottle on my chest. It's half full.

"I've never gone hunting—I've never killed something and eaten it before, not even a fish. I feel like I should do that. I've never fallen in love. I've never had sex," I admit.

Morgan is taking a drink as she receives this news, and sputters into the glass. "Seriously, never?"

"I've had girlfriends, and we fooled around—but, yeah. I don't know, I guess I am always about to move somewhere else, I didn't want anything serious."

"You don't need a serious relationship to have sex," Morgan tells me.

I can feel her staring at me, but I can't bring myself to look back. Instead, I unscrew the top from the bottle of scotch and put it to my lips. Warm, sharp liquor runs over my tongue, and I swallow. The next breath feels like fire.

Her statement floats somewhere between us, hovering, an awkward stranger.

She finishes off her glass. "I'm a person, Sean—even if I don't act like one. I'm lonely. I've been doing this for years. If I told you I've been to most of the museums in America, that I've been in a hotel room that cost two thousand dollars a night and spent another ten thousand on room service, that I've rented a Ferrari and driven naked across Death Valley, that I've read hundreds of books and seen a thousand movies, that I've camped out in the Everglades, that I've reeled in a shark, that—"

"Hold on. Why were you driving naked?" I laugh.

"You need to understand what it feels like to be on Italian leather seats," she supplies. "When it's a hundred degrees out, and there's no one around for hours, and you've got two hundred thousand dollars of engine roaring under you—" she pauses and exhales, as though breathless from recalling the memory. "It's good. Look, this life has more to offer than just scrambling to escape the police. It means you can be free in a way almost no one ever is. You can live without regard."

"Sounds nice," I say, turning away.

Her hand reaches out and lands on mine, which is wrapped around the bottle. And then we're touching, and my pulse is pounding.

More manipulation. Except, I can't move. Her hand is too warm, too soft, fingers tenderly clutching mine.

Morgan leans over, rests on the armrest, and brings herself closer. "There's no one to enjoy these things with," she says. Voice like melted butter. "Until now—if you want. If you're not so worried about being smarter than me."

Her lips are within reach; she's leaned halfway over to me. She exercises the privilege her power affords.

Can't—not sure what to do; my brain is in overload, words babbling into one another, coming out misshapen and bent. "Stop..." I mumble halfheartedly, deconstructed.

And she leans in, puts one hand on my chair, and presses her lips to mine. Soft, wet, warm—our lips move in concert, hesitantly at first, then not. Then, hungrily.

We kiss forever, but it ends instantly. Morgan pulls back. "It's a beautiful world, Sean Reilly," she says. As she collapses into her chair, the bottle of scotch goes with her.

27. What to do with everything

MAIN STREET, OCALA HAS A GIMMICK, a motif. Everything calls back to some idyllic pre-Civil War time that was probably never quite this graceful: stately plantation homes, mint sprigs in the sweet tea, and black men in white suits. The whole vaguely racist fantasy makes me uncomfortable.

"I can't believe *this* is how you wanted to spend your morning," Morgan says, walking slowly to keep pace with me as I hobble along.

"You said I could spend some money," I reply as I work my way down the sidewalk, *clack* of my crutches punctuating every step.

"I thought maybe you'd want to go to a strip club, or sip some hundred dollar wine in a fancy restaurant."

"I don't think I'd like a strip club," I say. "Sit in a crowded room with a bunch of strangers and do what? Talk about our hard-ons?"

Morgan laughs into her hand; gold bracelet and pale pink fingernails. They're painted to match her lips.

Those lips. Other than the kiss, nothing has happened. It established a truth, though: My knowledge that she's a master manipulator doesn't actually stop her from controlling me.

I spot my target—a worn bundle of a man, dusty baseball cap pulled over his eyes. A paper cup rests in his hands, and a cardboard sign scrawled with his plea is trapped under his foot. There are a few quarters in the coffer.

I bend over at the waist, as the cast won't allow me to squat—it appears I am bowing. The beggar snores softly; I pull five hundred dollars from my pocket and place it into his cup.

"Have a good day," I say loudly; he snorts awake. I stand immediately, motion for Morgan, and continue down the street.

"That's anticlimactic," she murmurs as we walk.

"Are you kidding? I feel awesome," I say, smiling.

About the time we turn the corner, the dusty man howls with joy.

I see Morgan smile out of my peripheral vision. She speaks: "I pick next."

I press the butt against the inside of my shoulder, then pull tight, line up the sights, and squeeze.

The rifle only makes a halfhearted pop, muted through the foam plugs pressed into my ears. Two more squeezes, and two more bullets pop off in quick succession. The paper target shudders slightly as holes are torn through it.

Two more pulls, two more holes in the target. The device is warm and alive, clean smell of oil and gunpowder lingering as I continue to fire. It operates flawlessly, as it should—it is a seven thousand dollar semiautomatic rifle modeled after something they use in the military. The whole thing is light; almost too light, so that I couldn't believe it was a real gun when the store's owner put it in my hands.

"That's pretty amazing," I half shout as I slide the empty clip from the gun, pull back the chamber, and place it on a table next to five more rifles of various size and complexity. We've been here at the gun range test-firing them all, so much that my shoulder aches and I'm sure it's bruised.

I don't think Morgan heard me; she's looking down the barrel of a tiny black revolver, firing shots every few seconds, steadily. She focuses on the target, squinting behind yellow tinted safety glasses. Five of the bullets land in a loose bundle around the target's center, with one having veered up to the side of the neck.

When she's finished, she turns and smiles. Morgan pulls the sound canceling headphones from her ears.

"Do you like it?" I ask.

"I'm buying two," she answers. "And one is for you. Here, take it."

"I don't want a gun," I say. "They're fun, I mean, this is fun—but I don't want to worry about shooting people."

Her eyebrows raise. "You shot Jack. I didn't think you had it in you. He didn't either, obviously, or he wouldn't have tried to run."

"That's different—he murdered Kayla."

"Someday, someone may want to murder you."

Morgan slides the cylinder out, then empties six casings into her hand. Her fingers close around them, and they rattle when she shakes her closed fist.

She stares into my eyes; I find myself paralyzed. While keeping this line between us alive, she prompts for me to take the gun. I am unable to refuse, and lift the unloaded weapon from her hand.

"It's heavy," I say.

A new energy fills Morgan: "You want heavy; you want to know it's there. Revolvers are best, because they don't leave shell casings. You don't want to try and pick those up in a hurry. Don't carry it everywhere, because you'll be in trouble if you get caught, at least until we can get you a permit. But, keep it near the money—you need to be able to defend the money. And, load it with different brands of shells, so if you do shoot someone, the police will look for multiple shooters. And never—" she glances up at me and smiles. "You'll be fine."

Morgan isn't giving me an option, and so I only nod. "What's for dinner?" I ask.

"We'll order takeout; I've got some plans for you at home."

"Plans?" I ask.

"You'll like it," she promises. "My hands will be all over you."

———— ✂ ————

Morgan drags her fingertips over the surface of my scalp, each follicle bending and twisting around her hands. I'm focused entirely on the feeling, and where her fingers are, so is my world.

"You've got goose bumps," she says.

I only groan softly. The skylight in our new kitchen glows red behind closed eyelids.

"Okay, now what's the trick to avoid carrying cash everywhere?" Morgan asks, quizzing me again.

"Pre-paid gift cards," I answer, voice a moan. "The kind credit card companies put out."

"And how do you buy those?"

"With cash."

"While wearing what?"

"A hat and sunglasses," I answer.

"Why?"

Her hands vanish for a moment, then return with force, hair dye wet and cold on my scalp. Morgan insisted I dye my hair, and we settled on blond.

I can't stand the look, but I see the logic. Between this and the new, colored contacts, I'm making myself that much harder to catch. A blond-haired, blue-eyed Sean Reilly. Not sure I like it; it makes me feel somehow less Irish.

"Most security cameras are overhead. Wearing a hat and sunglasses makes you hard to identify," I answer.

I do like the process of being dyed, though. A plastic comb runs through my hair, followed by her palm, which soothes my scalp after the black teeth rake over my skin.

While the dye sets, her thumbs press into my neck, kneading the muscles around my spine. This is not something that gets touched—maybe ever—and the feeling is overwhelming.

Maybe she's shaken an idea free, though, a bit of mischief. I decide to test her. "If I wanted to leave now, could I?"

Her hands stop moving. "Do you want to leave?"

"I've been thinking about it," I answer, voice glib.

"Stop it," she says, hands still rigid on my neck.

"What do you mean?" I ask, though my cheeks are already beginning to burn.

Her fingers fall away, hands landing at her sides. "Since we established that I'm manipulative, and I need you to be here right now, you think that by threatening to leave, you can drive me to do more to please you. But instead, I'm calling you out on it."

She's pulled the words out of my mind. I fall quiet.

What she says next is somewhere between a compliment and a condemnation: "You're learning fast."

28. My many faces

"SO I'M JUST GOING TO WALK IN and get a driver's license? Like Ryan White is a real person?" I ask Morgan, rubbing my palms on the leather seat of the car.

"Ryan White has all the qualifications of a real person," she tells me. "He has a birth certificate issued from a hospital nineteen years ago. He's had an email address for six years, a cell phone for five years, and a credit card for two. He enrolled in a high school—though you'll find he was tardy often. Okay, he never went to class. But he's got a real paper trail, and as far as the world of information is concerned, that makes him real. He just needs a face—yours."

"A face with stupid yellow hair," I add. I do not like looking in the mirror and seeing this person; it doesn't look like me. Sean Reilly would never dye his hair this color, or any color.

I suppose that's the point.

"Good luck," she calls as I open the car door, slide my crutches out and steady myself. I hobble across a freshly paved parking lot, smell of tar wet in my nose.

Strange, what makes a person. I'm dead, officially, with a closed file—and definitely feel real. Poor Ryan White here never lived a day of his life; he's only the shell of a human, waiting for a soul to animate him, and yet he's supposed to be alive.

There's no one to hold the door for me, and I struggle to stretch my crutches in ahead. When I'm inside, the wind slams the door into my back; I barely keep myself from falling over.

I'm basically a ballerina with these things.

After I check in, I find a chair in the corner and rest, eyes focused on the floor. Thoughts of Morgan flash through my mind; a hundred questions, desires. Then, that's probably what she wants. Or is it?

I've never met anyone like her. I still don't know if I've seen her, really, or if it's all been an act. Even when she burned the car, and smoked in front of me—her story didn't add up. I met Cole, and he was pissed. Outraged. It couldn't just be that she escaped him, not after all these years.

It's all manipulation, but it's enchanting to watch. Maybe that's all she is—mask after mask, infinitely reoccurring. Maybe that's still a special kind of person, though.

I rise when Ryan White's name is announced over the speaker. I step up to the desk of a dark-skinned woman with gold hoop earrings and a bored expression. I answer a few questions, then hand her the social security card, credit card, and forged form stating I passed Driver's Ed.

She directs me to a scotch-tape 'x' on the floor. I stand over it and look down the barrel of a camera. I don't smile, just stare. A bulb flashes, and my face appears on a monitor next to the woman.

"This all right?" she asks.

"Yes," I say, trying to hide my accent.

She prints out a temporary driver's license—the real one is being mailed to a post office box that Morgan and I rented with cash earlier today.

I take the form absentmindedly. I can't stop looking at myself in the computer monitor—the face staring back at me looks betrayed; the yellow hair is unorthodox, unwelcome.

No idea who I am anymore, and that's staring me right in the face.

29. Responsible living

W E RETURN TO FIND JACK in the kitchen. He's set up a scene—boxes are torn open below him, and he leans over a small bathroom heater. His thin, hairy legs jut from cargo shorts, and dusty feet are strapped into worn sandals. The bandage on his arm is new, professionally done, and looks clean.

The heater hums softly on the counter, and behind a thin grate, coils glow orange. An identical heater rests on the floor near his feet, though it isn't plugged in.

Without turning around to acknowledge us, Jack starts talking: "How do you start a fire in this day and age? The forensics are insane."

I examine the torn boxes to his right; they're shipping envelopes. Two textbooks are on the counter, one of them open. They're titled *Modern Forensics* and *Fire Investigator's Handbook*.

I take a seat across from Jack, on one of the kitchen stools, and join him in watching the heater. It seems like an average little device, a white plastic cube with knobs on top.

"Cigarettes and matchbooks?" I ask, remembering the trick Morgan showed me with the car.

"Not even close," he says, then takes a long sniff. "That's obvious arson, it just lets you put distance between yourself and the fire. This can't look like anyone set the fire on purpose, or it won't be an accidental death." He pauses. "You smell that?"

I smell nothing. "No."

"Might be my imagination. Morgan, you smell anything?" he calls. She rests on one of the recliners, facing a cold fireplace.

She says nothing.

Jack runs a hand down his face. "You can't start the fire, that's the problem. They can see if you use gasoline, lighter fluid, anything. It shows you, right in that book. After everything is burned, it's pretty obvious. Big streaks in the ground where the gas is lit. Basically, they're going to figure out how your fire started, no matter what you do."

"So, don't use a fire," I say.

"The fire is for bonus points," he mutters.

The heater grunts softly. Jack hops back, hands shooting out, framing the device.

Nothing happens.

"I give," I say. "What's the deal with the heater?"

Jack grins. "It's been recalled, about five years ago. I found these two on eBay. The thing's defective, or so I'm told. It's supposed to catch fire if you leave it on this setting. If this works, that's my natural fire. My accident. When the cops investigate, they'll decide Ronald Silver has been murdered by a bad heater. Chalk it up to bad luck."

I wave my hands dismissively, then turn and look over the living room. Morgan rests on the recliner, both hands folded on her chest, black spaghetti strap top feeding into a charcoal skirt. She picks at a painted fingernail repeatedly, though from here, it appears flawless.

"Ah-hah!" Jack shouts triumphantly. An orange flame flickers within the heater's enclosure, half hidden by the metal grate. In moments, the acrid stench of burning plastic fills the living room, and I'm forced to rise and back away.

"Would you unplug it now?" Morgan calls, voice angry.

"Sorry; got to see how high the flame goes," Jack says, picking up a slim cardboard shipping box and fanning the fumes away from his face. "Maybe I could have done this outside."

I start heading toward my room, though when I'm near the hallway, I turn. "I don't get it," I call to Jack. "What are they going to think happened to his body? I mean, you've got to have one, right? And it's not like it can be Ronald Silver, he isn't even real."

Jack looks at me over the warped monstrosity on the table—cream colored plastic writhing in bubbling agony, orange flame streaming black smoke. When our eyes connect, I can only turn away.

"You'll see," he says.

30. Faking a life

"THANKS FOR BREAKFAST," I murmur, wiping my hands on the single paper napkin included in our sack full of breakfast tacos.

"No problem," Morgan responds.

I stare out the window at an overgrown field, last vestiges of wildflowers wilting under the arrival of summer. A herd of cattle congregate under the shade of a single oak tree, bodies pressed to the cool earth.

We drive for fifteen minutes, leaving Ocala proper and traveling down the poorly paved farm roads that form a grid across the county. We pass a dilapidated southern estate which lies in ruin, a pillar fallen across the entryway, cracked under its own weight.

We reach a small trailer park, fenced in by barbed wire and blanketed by soft red sand. Fresh signs warn us to obey the speed limit. The lot is mostly empty—only a handful of RV's and mobile homes. However, what's here seems expensive, with glistening paint and thin carbon-black satellite dishes.

Morgan parks in front of a shining new RV, obnoxious tribal design sweeping across the gleaming metal panels.

"This is Jack's?" I ask.

She shakes her head. "Ronald Silver's."

I follow her across the red dirt, crutches sliding just enough to unnerve me. She knocks on the door of the Winnebago, eliciting a hollow, metallic sound.

The door opens to a bleary eyed, hollow cheeked Jack. He stands in the frame, holding a rag to his face, about an inch from his nose. He inhales, moans sharply, and motions for us to come inside. Jack collapses back on a plastic bench; the flask of ether sits on the table next to him.

The air conditioner blasts full throttle, and cool air feels crisp on my skin. The interior is half leather—real or not—and half cloth, everything a light cream color. Tables and chairs line the walls, and a television has risen from a wooden dresser.

Jack puts an arm down on the table, then attempts to hold his chin—except he slips, and only just stops himself from banging his head. Dozens of printed forms are spread out in front of him, and a black pen rests uncapped on the table.

"These are hard," he says simply, slapping his hand down on the papers.

"The ether is helping you concentrate, then?" Morgan remarks.

"I was up all night," he groans. "My arm hurts. I didn't think there would be this much paperwork. Could you?" He holds up the pen, offering it to her.

Morgan clucks her tongue, sighs, but walks to the table and sits down. She rearranges the documents, painted fingernails clicking against the polished table as she collects the papers in a stack and rotates them to face her.

I lean against the wall and scratch idly under my cast. With time to spare, my eyes wander the mobile home, trying to piece together the story.

Creating a life. Travel booklets from all around the United States and Canada are spread across the passenger seat of the giant van. The trashcan is full: trays from microwaved dinners, cigar rings, and the discarded packaging from some pill that promises to make its purchaser 'twice the man.' Two posters of scantily clad women in provocative positions decorate the walls near the bathroom.

"Did you just spend a few days here and it looks like this, or is there a reason for it?" I ask Jack.

Morgan snorts out a laugh.

Jack answers: "Arrested development. Older guy, briefly married, now widowed, never matured. Spends his considerable wealth on big toys that he thinks will get him laid, which is what he really wants. Of course, those of us on the outside can see that his personality means he won't get it unless he pays for it. Check in the glove compartment; it's a masterstroke."

I open the glove compartment. A few sections of newspaper are stuffed inside: the classifieds from different dates. I shuffle through; some parts are circled in red ink. Thinly veiled advertisements for prostitutes.

I close the glove box and turn around. At the opposite end of the narrow chamber is the second of the two defective bathroom heaters. It sits beneath a small wicker table. This is Jack's fire-starting setup.

A stack of magazines rest on the table above the heater, and thick cotton curtains stretch down from the nearest window to meet them. A clear path for the fire, from the heater to the ceiling.

Morgan stares at one of the documents, then squints. After a moment, she picks up her purse from the floor and begins rifling through it. As the seconds pass, she begins to do so violently, hand tearing through the bag. Eventually, she stops and curses. "I left the social security card. I need the number to fill this out."

"Rookie," Jack grins from his position slumped over in the chair.

"This is going to take hours. Sean, would you go grab the manila folder under my mattress? Not the redwell or the beige binder, but the manila folder."

"Got a lot of secrets under that bed?" Jack asks, voice slurred to near incoherency.

Morgan only casts him a sideways glance, then throws the keys to me.

"I'll be right back," I promise.

I hobble out to the car, taking my time to put the crutches in the back seat. The car is an automatic, thankfully, and so I can drive with only one good leg. I take my time adjusting the mirrors in the car—can't afford to be pulled over.

Cautious driving brings me home; I pull all the way into the driveway and turn off the car. After I shuffle to the front door, it takes me a moment to find the right key. The deadbolt slides open with a well-oiled clack.

The keychain rattles as it presses between my palm and the foam pad of the crutches. I drop the keys on the kitchen table, then move to the living room.

I hear the intruder a split second before I'm shoved to the floor. I stumble forward, press my broken leg into the ground automatically. The pain is blinding, flash bang grenade in my skull —I fall, hands pressed to the cold tile floor. My crutches clatter, one within reach, one not.

I turn to see Cole, both hands gripping a gun that's pointed at my chest.

31. I blinked

I CRAWL BACK ON MY ELBOWS—anything to put distance between us.

"What do you want?" I ask. My voice quakes out, sound waves jagged, betraying my terror.

"You look an awful lot like Sean Reilly," he says. "You know, the dead murderer?"

It's Cole—squinty-eyed and beer-gutted, clad in a plaid shirt and blue jeans, brown leather belt and black boots. Bothers me that they don't match.

His gut deforms the shirt, balloons it around his waist until it comes tightly cinched at his hips, tucked into a pair of jeans. Nervous, tired look. Eyes sunken, mustache graying. I can smell him from here.

"And that's the punishment for looking like someone else? You kick them over? I've got a broken leg."

Cole huffs out a single chuckle. "Cut the shit, kid. Where is she?"

"I don't know what you're talking about."

He shakes the gun, takes a step closer. I crawl backward, but press against a granite pillar which separates the living room from the hallway. Nowhere to go.

"Where's Lauren?"

"I don't know anyone named Lauren," I answer. Is that Morgan's real name?

"You know who I'm talking about. I know they helped you fake your death. Listen, I have no problem killing you, like you killed that girl. They find your body, they aren't going to search very hard for who did it." He waves the pistol between my head and chest as he threatens me.

I pull one of the crutches closer with my foot, until I can reach it. Once it's in hand, I talk: "Listen, I'll talk to you. How about I sit down in a chair? My leg feels like shit." With one palm on the ground and another on my crutch, I begin pulling myself up. "I can't even walk. What am I going to do?"

Cole doesn't disagree, or shoot me—I take this as a sign I can pull myself the rest of the way up. I do so, peripheral vision straining to track the gun.

"Why do you want her so bad?" I ask, limping on one crutch over to the brown recliner and falling into it.

"Why do I—why do I want to find her so bad?" He gestures as he talks, and the tip of the pistol waves with his words. I imagine a laser-thin red line pointing from the barrel, and track it as the gun moves, cowering inwardly when the line crosses my body. "She took my baby from me."

"What?"

He laughs humorlessly. "You don't know anything, do you?"

"What the hell are you talking about?"

"I mean when she 'died,'" he forms quotes around this word, "she was eight months pregnant."

This is news.

"What do you think happened to my child when she disappeared? I'd love to know. It could be out there somewhere, if that whore didn't kill it!" While he talks, the weapon trembles.

My voice is low: "I don't know anything about that. I haven't known her long, and she's always been nice to me."

"She would be friends with a murderer, wouldn't she?" he asks.

"I'm not a murderer," I tell him. "It's complicated."

"You confessed!"

"I'm not..." I stop. Pointless to try and convince him. "How did you even find us?"

Cole smirks. "Tips come in from all over the country with your name on them—course, no one else knows who you're traveling with. After you three got pulled over in Lake Charles, it wasn't too hard to track you from there. Now, call her. Make her come back here. Your life for her life, that's the only deal I'm going to make."

I reach into my jeans pocket; the prepaid phone is a blocky plastic clamshell, and wouldn't have been impressive ten years ago. I flip it open. Morgan's latest cell phone number is in my call history; I find it and press the button.

"Don't tell her I'm here," Cole says. "Tell her to come, and that's it." He stands next to me as I dial, gun just out of reach.

The phone rings once, and Morgan answers.

"Where are you?" she asks.

"Listen close," I say. "I'm at the house. Cole is here, he's got a gun."

The phone flies from my hand as a fist connects with my jaw; I see stars. He leans over me and strikes again, from the other side. This one hurts worse than the first, and before my vision clears, the taste of blood fills my mouth.

"You think you're smart, don't you?" he asks. He clutches my bad leg and pulls; the cast absorbs most of the stress, but the movement on my broken knee is torture. I'm dragged off the sofa and land on the floor; he yanks the crutch from my hands and hurls it across the room.

A boot rushes at my face. I lift my arms up, catching his shin with my forearms. The stitches of his shoe scrape my cheek; he pulls back to kick again. As I struggle to get out of the way, I hook my good leg behind the one he's balanced on, and pull as hard as I can.

Cole comes crashing down, falling back on his ass. The gun is still in his hand, pointing at the ceiling as he topples. Immediately I lunge at him, pushing off my good leg and landing on top of the bigger, heavier man.

Both of my hands are on the gun as I work to stay on top, knee on the soft center of his body. He curses, clawing at my chest then clutching my throat with his free hand. As he squeezes, I take one hand from the gun and punch him in the side of the head—once, twice, then as I bring my fist back a third time, he shifts his weight and I fall to the side.

We lay side by side, fighting for the weapon. His fist slams into my chest repeatedly, making hollow thumping sounds. The third hit is too much; I flinch involuntarily, pulling my hands back to my body and letting go of the gun.

He springs up, panting, wet with sweat. I move after him, but am too slow, and by the time I'm halfway to my feet I'm staring at the sight on his gun.

"Tell me why I shouldn't kill you now," Cole huffs. Buttons across his shirt are ripped out; one hangs limp by a thread across his hairy chest.

I wipe my forearm across my mouth, and see skin streaked with blood.

I'm probably about to die, I realize. Really die.

Well, at least everyone already thinks I'm dead. That's most of it, right there. My stadium full of people came and went; everyone else's pain is covered—all that's left is mine. Just the immediate, visceral sensation of my life draining away.

I just stare at the gun.

Cole grunts, holds the pistol steady at my head, but doesn't fire. A drop of sweat rolls down his forehead, and his tongue sticks out the side of his mouth to catch it.

"You think she'll come?" he asks.

"I hope she'll run," I answer.

32. Reunited

TIME SPENT WITH A GUN pointed at my head is not like normal time. It passes in increments that shouldn't be defined as "seconds," because that implies each interval can be measured separately from the rest. This is a tumbling stream of cubed moments, a shambling mess of static and broken thoughts. The mass of these will sit in my memory like hot coals, untouchable and immovable, scarred into my experience.

Cole and I stand, sweating, rubbing the wounds we've inflicted on each other. Occasionally, between heaving breaths, he shakes the gun and jabs it in my direction, like he's going to shoot. The panic this generates in my mind is so consuming, I have to look down and check my clothes to make sure I'm not shot.

At some point, we hear a car pull into the driveway. Cole keeps the gun pointed in my general direction as he walks to the living room window, pulls back the curtain and stares outside. I consider running, but the pain in my skull and leg dissuade me.

Can't see from here, but I hear the faint *thud* of a car door slamming, then the jingle of keys as someone approaches the door. Cole walks over and opens it before the keys are turned.

He steps back, and Morgan enters the house—silent, face ashen, black purse tucked under one arm. Gleaming black shoes emerge from granite slacks and tap the ground with authority.

Cole lets the gun fall to his side, seemingly staggered. His eyes are wide, mouth open, skin sickly pale behind splotch-pink blemishes.

"I mean, I knew," Cole stammers. "I was pretty goddamn sure you were alive, you know. But seeing you...I spent years thinking you're dead, then the past year convinced I'm crazy for thinking you might be alive." He raises spread fingers to his head, touches his forehead and pushes the hand outward.

"You're right here. That's you, that's my Lauren. The woman who ruined my life!" He shouts this as he holds the gun sideways and levels it at her chest. He's a few feet away, pistol halving the distance between them.

Morgan only stares, unflinching. "Shoot me and lose your son forever," she says.

Cole bends over as though struck again, but keeps the gun pointed at Morgan. "It's a boy?" he croaks.

"A healthy three year old," Morgan answers. She hooks the purse around her arm, holds it near her body. "He's somewhere safe, leading a pampered life."

"We tried for years to get you pregnant, and you stole him! All you ever want is to hurt me," Cole says, voice ragged.

Morgan doesn't respond to this.

I sense motion in my peripheral vision; the moment before I turn to glance, Morgan's eyes flit to mine. She says nothing, but I remain still. Something passes by the glass panes in the back door, momentarily blocking the sun.

"What's his name?" Cole calls, straightening himself out again.

She's still silent. Her face is porcelain, but there's a sheen to her eyes. A wet light.

"Tell me his name!" Cole shouts.

The back door opens, silently, slowly. Jack emerges, crouches low and pulls himself behind a half-wall that divides the kitchen. The door hangs slightly open.

Morgan's voice cracks, and a single tear tumbles to the floor. "I want to be with him too, Cole. But I can't, not with my life like this." She stares down for a moment, then sniffs wetly and runs a clenched hand under the offending eye which leaked the tear.

He seems to soften at this. "Then let's go together. Let's go get our son, Lauren. Come home to me."

Morgan's face craters with emotion, dimples tightened and lips pressed to one another. "It's all been a big mess. We can go together, I'm tired of running. I want to be with him."

Cole half-laughs, crying now. "You know I don't believe that," he says.

I almost can, for a second. Something in her voice.

"He could be in your arms tomorrow," Morgan says softly. "Even if you find him without me, it will take years to do the paperwork, to do the paternity test. With me, he could be yours instantly."

Cole chuckles humorlessly. "I'd be an idiot to trust you."

"Then don't," she answers, voice dead. "Arrest me, I don't care. I miss my son. Nothing is worth being separated from him."

The weapon dips, rises, then dips again, falling to his hip. "I'm taking you up on that." His voice is hoarse, traumatized smile forced onto his face.

Cole pulls a leather holster from his pocket, places it over the gun, and hooks this into the small of his back. After a dig through his pockets, he produces a pair of handcuffs.

But by the time he's completed this motion, Morgan's purse hits the floor. Cole looks up from the black leather bag to her hand, which clutches a snubnosed revolver. It's aimed at his head.

Morgan's emotion-wracked face is wiped clean, a fresh mask in place. She looks to the darkened space where Jack hides, and nods. He emerges, crouching low, bundle of rags in hand. The stick-thin man moves in soft bounds, taking big steps on the balls of his feet.

By the time Cole turns, one of Jack's arms is around his neck, and the other is pressing a wad of rags to his mouth. Cole struggles, arms flailing even as he keeps his eyes on the weapon in Morgan's hand.

Cole's shouts are muffled through the wet rags. He spins, but Jack leaps on his back. Cole stumbles to one knee; Jack pushes his legs into the ground and lunges forward, toppling the sheriff and dragging him down. They become a tangled mess of arms and legs, neither distinguishable from the other.

Gradually, though, one set of limbs slow. Cole's shouts slur into a long moaning syllable. His hand taps weakly at Jack's forearm, then finally falls to the floor with a hollow smack. Cole's gun is pulled from its place in his pants; Jack slides it across the stone floor.

Jack rises and wipes his hands on his jeans. The shirt is half-pulled from his chest, collar distended, and sweat covers his face. He lifts the ether-soaked rags and takes a quick whiff, whimpers, then leans down and presses the rags back to Cole's drooling mouth.

"We can use him," Jack says. "It'll be perfect."

Morgan lowers her gun. She hesitates a moment, considering something. Then: "Do it. What about the one you've already got?"

Jack sighs slowly, gazing at nothing. "We'll ditch it. This is better—he's still breathing." Then he barks an empty laugh. "Wonder if I can get a refund."

Then they both turn and stare at me. I'm missing something, and I don't know what, and it's apparent they're aware of this.

"Get him out of here," Jack says to Morgan.

She hesitates, then nods.

"What?" I asked. "Where do I go? Why?"

"I'll tell you after," Morgan says, walking over to Cole. His eyes open, bleary, and he moans. An arm twitches off the floor, seeming to rise after Morgan's leg. Halfway there, though, it falls back to the tile.

She walks to the window, peers down the street. "He drove here. Check his pockets, please."

Jack does so, kicking the moaning man's hands out of the way and reaching into his blue jeans. Keys emerge, jingling. "Says Dodge," he remarks.

Morgan nods, then walks to the table and picks up the keys to the Mercedes. She flings these at me; they bounce off my chest and land on the ground, where I pick them up.

"Take our car someplace quiet, and wait there until I call you," she orders. "And whatever you do, under no circumstances are you to open the trunk. Do you understand?"

I just nod.

"Go!" she commands again. "Go now." Then she sees the look in my eyes, and softens for a moment. "I'll explain when there's time. I promise."

33. The passenger

SOMETHING SLIDES AROUND IN THE TRUNK every time I turn or stop. It sounds soft and heavy—I don't like this sound; it's oddly familiar.

I drive the streets of Ocala for about an hour, finding something wrong with any space I might park and hide in. I constantly check my speed, hitting the brakes when I realize I'm over the limit.

Something's happening. Jack and Morgan abducted Cole, and I don't know what they're planning. Don't know what to think, and that not-knowing crackles through me—a spark in my blood that won't die down. It just sizzles, circulating.

My face hurts, and I have a headache. My lip is still bleeding. Never had a gun in my face. Never wrestled for my life before. And Morgan's kid—what's the truth? She certainly left that out of her sob story to me. Is Cole as bad as she makes him out to be, or is that a lie, too?

My phone buzzes; I check it. A text from Morgan:

Come to the trailer park, wait outside.

I make my way out of Ocala toward the little rural development. After I park on the side of the small farm road that connects to the trailer park, there is nothing to do but wait.

It's only a few minutes before I see two figures, male and female, walking toward me. Jack in a red hoodie, hands tucked into the pocket at its center, and Morgan in charcoal slacks and a teal blouse. Clothes whip like shrouds in the wind, constant eastbound motion tugging them off their path.

Nothing seems particularly urgent about the way they move. However, a thin stream of black smoke rises from somewhere deeper within the park.

I get out of the car, not even bothering with my crutches, but instead using the vehicle to support my weight as I hop to the back seat and open it. By the time I slide back into my spot, Jack opens the driver's side and climbs in.

Morgan, however, doesn't follow. Instead, she walks around to my window, and motions for me to roll it down. I do.

"I need to ditch Cole's car," she says. Her voice is tired, and wind whips the tips of her dark hair against her neck and face. "Stay with Jack."

"How about Jack hides the truck, and you come with me?" I ask.

I don't get a response—just a look that tells me not to argue.

"Let me come with you in Cole's car, then!" I call at her back.

"It involves a hike." I barely hear her; she's already halfway across the road again. The thin stream of smoke rising from the trailer park grows to a thicker column, hooking up and to the right as wind drags it away from its source.

I roll the window back up.

"We've got a present to return," Jack tells me.

I say nothing as he pulls a U-turn and begins driving back toward Ocala.

Rice fields surround us, saturated in a few inches of water, and the shallow pools glitter in the sunlight. Sprouts shoot up in patches, breaking the gleaming baldness of their surfaces.

"You guys killed Cole, didn't you?" I ask. I lean my head against the hot window and stare at the rubber lining where glass meets metal.

Jack checks his wristwatch. "By now, probably." He glances back at me. "What, you feel bad?"

"He was going to shoot me," I say, aware I'm rationalizing it.

Jack chuckles. "You do feel bad. What's that like?"

"It hurts."

He starts to respond, then looks back at me and seems to reconsider. After a moment, he starts again: "I mean, he probably didn't suffer. We gave him a lot of ether; he'll suffocate before he burns to death. Cole won't even know he's dead."

That doesn't make me feel much better. But, it's not like I killed him. Not like there's any other way. Right?

Jack, on the other hand, seems chipper. He taps his thumbs on the steering wheel, then accelerates into a turn so that the back wheels spin to the side as he brings the car around.

"And he really beat Morgan?"

"I've seen the bruises," he calls back, glancing into the rearview mirror. "She was a completely different person back then. Scared of everything. There was no division between her and her shadow; Morgan didn't realize she could be someone else. I freed her."

"You have an easy time killing people, don't you?" I ask.

Jack shrugs. "Murder." He sneers the word. "Murder is a human thing, it's an idea. I don't care about ideas. Animals kill, they don't murder. And the whole business is so conceptual anyway. Most of the people I kill never existed in the first place, you know, like Ronald Silver. Murder is something a prosecutor charges you with, it's a concept."

"Except when you murder a person like Cole or Kayla, that person doesn't get to exist anymore," I say.

"Yeah, but that's just one person."

"You're just one person, Jack."

We follow the road through an increasingly frequent set of traffic lights, convenience stores and fast food restaurants. We cross into the outer layers of Ocala.

A dim, cluttered gas station with fresh paint—tired employee sucking a cigarette next to the dumpster, a brief moment to be herself. Taco huts turn to fried chicken, to waffle houses, and by the time we're nearly to downtown, an Italian restaurant—rose red roof on a pink building.

Jack begins cursing. "Goddamnit. Knew it was too soon, they must be looking for the car."

I twist and look out the rear window. A police cruiser trails us, lights flashing, black grill caging chrome bumper.

"What the hell?" I ask.

"I blinked. Act normal," Jack instructs. "I don't have a driver's license. And, I'm not insured. And, we might be completely screwed, here."

This does not inspire confidence.

Jack pulls to a stop in the shoulder of the road. Faces in passing cars turn to stare at us; I search the interior of the car as though I'll find some escape hatch to deliver me from this situation.

The cop's door opens and he steps out. Beige uniform, black cap pulled low, silver star embroidered in its center. Not even a person, but a symbol of something I fear.

Jack rolls down his window as the man leans down and sticks his face in it.

"License and registration," he says, voice gruff.

"Can I ask what I did?"

"License and registration," he repeats.

"That's the thing, officer," Jack says. There's a little tremor in his tone, something I never heard before. "I just borrowed my friend's car so I could pop out to get a bite to eat, I don't have any paperwork on me."

"Step out of the car, sir," the officer says. He glances back at me, but seems uninterested. "Sir, do you mind if I look around the car?"

"Can I ask why?" Jack asks.

"Because this car is registered to a woman named Sarah Feisel. Are you Sarah Feisel?" he asks.

Jack shakes his head. "I know her, though. I just spoke to her ten minutes ago—do you want me to call her for you?"

The officer doesn't answer, but instead opens the rear door next to me. "You mind stepping out of the car as well?" he asks me.

I point at my broken leg, then nod in agreement. Something softens around his eyes as he watches me; he takes my crutches and holds them as I climb out. I make a show of wincing in pain as I rise, then take them from him.

"You okay?" he asks.

I only nod, certain the terror I'm feeling is evident on my face. Life in prison, the death penalty. It's all real again. I thought I could run, but there's no escape. It's like Morgan said: blink once, and they're on you.

"Did he hurt you?" the officer asks.

I only shake my head, afraid to let my accent be known. The look I get from him isn't suspicious, though. He seems worried about me.

That's fine. I'm worried about me, too. Ryan White's identification is in my pocket, but how long will that fool anyone?

The policeman leads Jack and me to the side of the road, and tells us to remain still while he searches. He paws under the seats, then between them, then through the glove box.

"What's in the trunk?" I ask quietly, not turning to look at Jack.

"The end of the line," he answers. His face has lost its color, and skin that was already pale has turned a light shade of green. "Y'know, since training you is going so well, here's a lesson: we should have switched cars again. There's always something to overlook. *Sarah Feisel.* I thought that name was clear."

"She used that name to bail me out of jail."

"Then that's why we're fucked," Jack says. "I put the car in her name."

The officer leans down under the driver's side dash and looks for the trunk release; he pulls it, and it pops open an inch. The cop walks around, puts both hands on the trunk, and lifts.

He looks down, then glances at us, then back at his cruiser. He leans forward, digs inside. Between the passing cars, I hear the sound of a zipper being pulled.

"Holy shit!" he shouts, taking two steps back, hand on his gun. Rather than going back to the trunk, he turns immediately to Jack and I. "Stay right there. Don't you move."

"What is it?" I ask.

"Yeah, what it is?" Jack asks as the policeman approaches.

He moves to Jack, grabs his left arm then steps behind him. As handcuffs click, I hobble a step forward and crane my neck so I can just see into the back of the car.

Protruding from a black canvas bag is the bald, bloodless face of a very dead man.

34. Belly

JACK IS LED to the back of the man's police car, and placed inside. "Do I need to put a pair of these on you?" the cop asks, returning with a second set of handcuffs. Sound waves wash over us as cars pass; he fights to keep his voice over the break.

I shake my head 'no.'

"Okay, just stand real still, I've got to check your pockets. It's just to make sure you don't have any guns or drugs. That okay? Nothing in there that's going to stick me, no needles or knives?"

"No," I say. He rifles through my pockets, retrieving my phone and ID. The ID he hands back, but the phone stays in his hand.

"Only until we're done talking," he says. "How do you know this man? Did you know there was a dead body in the trunk?"

"I didn't know about the body," I say finally, words wobbling through the air, broken arrows.

"Did he beat you up?" the officer asks, pointing at the side of my head. In the excitement, I forgot about the damage Cole did. I must look like hell: split lip, bruised face, dark marks on my arms where I tried to defend myself.

Instead of answering, I just stare at Jack in the back of the cruiser.

"It's okay, you don't have to tell me here. Where are your parents?" he asks.

I can't think of a good answer. "I don't..." My sentence is shaken apart by a cresting wave of panic. There is a corpse in the car; they aren't going to let me go. Eventually, they'll work out who I am. I'm going to prison forever.

So I just look down, glad for once to have crutches, because my good knee is weak.

Instead of pressing harder, though, the cop just nods knowingly. We stare at the ground together for at least a full minute.

Something catches my eye, and we both turn our heads. Two patrol cars arrive, one after the other, blue and white disco blitzkrieg.

The policeman who arrested Jack leans in close, speaks gently: "We need to hear exactly what happened, okay? I'm going to put you in the back seat of that patrol car, and he's going to drive you to the police station. You aren't under arrest, we just want to talk to you. But, that man *is* under arrest, and he's not going anywhere. So you're safe."

I nod again, hesitant, then pull myself forward with the crutches. Seems unreal that I'm moving freely, and I hesitate, half expecting to be tackled.

He looks at me, smiles, mutters an encouragement. This is the friendliest anyone's been to me in weeks.

I pass Jack on the way to my escort; he looks like he's in another place already. The eyes gleam, but there's nothing behind them. None of the hungry, half-mad weight that defined him.

The passenger door is opened for me, and I climb into the back of a police cruiser for the second time in my life.

There's still a chance. Maybe. The way it looks—me beaten up, in the back seat, with a broken leg. Plus, Jack is older, and he was driving. To these police, maybe I'm a victim and not a fugitive.

Just have to keep it that way.

———————— ✄ ————————

The police don't talk with me right away—they stick me in an empty conference room, where I sit at a big wooden table surrounded by worn office chairs. A whiteboard on the wall is blank, save the faint orange stains of markers that haven't quite washed away.

A television sits on a rack at the far end of the room, and the policeman gave me the remote before he sat me in here. I don't turn it on, though. I need time to think.

When I speak with the police, each consecutive word decides my fate. I must perform perfectly. I must craft a story—but there are so many details to take into account, so much I can't control. It's like throwing sewing needles into the air and threading them before they reach the ground.

I remember my interview with Detective Alvarado, and try to use it to prepare me now. He liked facts and evidence; he wanted me to tell a lie so he could present proof I lied. Once that happened, it was over.

Can't give them anything to hang me with.

I'm sure the reason I haven't been interviewed is that they're talking to Jack. Another variable I can't control—he could turn on me any moment.

But what if he keeps his mouth shut? It's a possibility. That body in the car must be the one he planned to use before Cole came along. He must not have murdered him, so he might not spend his whole life in prison. Jack could be in damage control mode, trying to limit his jail time.

Could be. I feel decidedly screwed, hanging my survival on guessing what a complete psychopath will do.

Well, maybe I should turn on him. I'm the one who looks abused—I can say Jack beat me up, made me come with him.

There is a pad on the table, and a pen with it. I uncap the cheap, black Bic and draw a large hash sign on the paper, a grid with nine spaces. Into the top left corner of the figure, I place the letter X.

If Jack realizes I turned on him, he might get even. Tell them my real name. One search of the web, and I'll be here for a long time. He'll do anything if he thinks it might help him, I've seen that.

I draw an O in the top right corner of the tic-tac-toe board. That's his move in the game, his reaction.

If he did that, I could tell the police he's Jack Vickery, and he killed Kayla. I could flip this on him, bring the whole thing around. Just maybe, I could be Sean Reilly again.

That thought makes me pause. What if I fixed everything? What if somehow I turned the tables, and I went home to Ireland again, and saw my parents? God, what a dream. Daring to think that draws a pang of desire. Mom's face. Not running anymore, but a normal teenager with a real life.

I place an X into the bottom left corner of the board, so only a third mark in the center is needed to complete my line.

But if I did that, Jack could point out that I wrote a confession, and went to great lengths to escape the law. After all, I already admitted to helping Kayla fake her death—facts which make me seem like an accomplice, or worse yet, the real killer. And who knows if the police can even connect him to the name 'Jack Vickery?'

An O is entered between the two Xs. It must play out that way—Jack won't let me sit here and blame everything on him. The harder I fight, the harder he will fight back.

I place Xs and Os in quick succession, imagining a battle in the courts, playing fairly for each side, attacking and reacting. In moments, the board is full, and both sides have tied. No one wins.

Really, it doesn't even matter if Jack turns on me first, or me on him, because the outcome will be the same: everyone will go to prison.

Here's the kick in the teeth, though—if Jack turns on me, and I don't do anything? I'll end up with all of it. Just like him, I have to defend if I'm attacked. But, I may not find out what he says—I'll just have to guess whether he ratted me out or not. So, how do I trust the murderer who got me here in the first place?

35. The MAD doctrine

NOTHING TO DO BUT COUNT MY BREATH and wait. I try to remain calm, because I know I'll need to be when the time comes. Can't get excited and blurt something out; I could ruin everything.

Have to do better than the last time I was in a police station.

It's almost an hour before a heavyset black man in a white polo shirt and tan slacks steps into the room and shuts the door behind him. I start to push myself up out of the chair to shake his hand.

"No, no, that's all right," he says quickly, voice low, waving his hands at me. "I insist, not with that broken leg and everything."

He stands motionless, watching me for a couple of seconds, until I'm completely relaxed back into my seat—only then does he reanimate.

His hand juts out, dark with gnarled knuckles. "I'm Detective Green," he says. "But you can call me Charlie."

We shake hands. His grip is solid, but he doesn't squeeze my hand. He's got the dial switched over to 'comforting.'

"Hi, Charlie," I say. "I'm Ryan." I keep my voice quiet, my eyes on the floor.

Charlie sits down in the chair next to me and rests one elbow on the table. "You look like you're having a bad day," he says, still genial, like a nice uncle you only see at holidays.

The corner of my upper lip jerks into a half-smile for a second, then collapses under the strain. "I've had better."

"That's some accent. Where are you from, Ryan?"

"I'm from Scotland," I answer.

"And where are your parents, Ryan? We checked through your phone—I hope you don't mind—and we checked the phone books, but we're having trouble finding them."

I stare down at the table, at the tic-tac-toe board that embodies my dilemma. "My parents are dead. They died in the same crash I broke my leg in," I answer. "Back in Scotland. But I was born here, and I spent about half my life in Florida, with my grandparents. I have a cousin here, so I came here to reunite and stay with her. There's nothing left for me in Edinburgh."

"I'm very sorry to hear that, Ryan. So you lost your parents recently? I know that can hurt. My dad died last year." He practically sings the words, voice dripping sympathy.

When I don't offer anything else, an uncomfortable silence fills the room. I swallow back the urge to tell him my real name, to spill everything. Kayla's real murderer is in a cell somewhere in this police station, and I only need to say so to put him away.

Instead, I force a weak smile.

"How did you wind up in that car today?" he asks me.

One thought repeats in my head, over and over again: What did Jack tell them? If he already told them everything, and I sit here and play innocent, I'm only going to look guilty. The best time to strike would be now, while I have the chance to prove I'm the victim. Now, while they still trust me.

Unless Jack hasn't talked. If he hasn't, I'd only be starting a war I can't finish.

"I landed in Orlando a few weeks ago, and stayed in a hotel. There's a little money from their life insurance, you know. It took me a while to find Cassandra—that's my cousin—on Facebook. She sent that guy to come get me."

"What's his name?" he asks.

"No one's told me," I answer.

"That's an hour and a half drive. He didn't tell you his name?" Now the syrupy pretense is gone. Just skepticism.

"We didn't get along very well. He seemed real pissed about having to pick me up."

"Did he beat you up?" the detective asks, pointing at his own face to demonstrate the damage to mine.

I turn and look at the wall, pressing my lips together. A few seconds pass.

"If he did, we can file assault charges."

The lies develop quickly in my head. Everything unverifiable, everything loose. Point him at a patch of shadows. "I'm trying to stay with my cousin," I say. "That's her boyfriend. If I start trouble, there won't be anywhere for me to live."

"Well, Ryan, there's a dead body in the trunk of his car. You think she's still going to want to stay with him once she hears that?" He folds his hands on his lap. There's some new age symbol in silver on his middle finger.

"Did he murder someone?" I ask. "Was he going to murder me?"

The detective shrugs. "That's what I'm trying to find out."

"I saw the body. What happened to that man?"

He rubs the back of his neck. "We're not sure. There wasn't any blood, there aren't any injuries. Been dead for a while. Nobody is missing who fits that description. He's just...dead."

I nod. Confirms what I guessed about the body. If that's true, maybe Jack won't spend much time in prison. Good for me—gives him a reason not to talk.

"I don't know who that was," I answer. "That's scary. I rode in that car a few feet away from a dead body."

Detective Green leans back and sighs, then raps his fingers across the table. He watches me for a moment, and I remain still, counting my breath.

Not sure if this is working.

"Did he say anything about being from Texas?" the detective asks me.

Suddenly I'm light-headed; the blood drains from my face, and with it, the color drains from the world—washed out from the top down.

Texas. They know about Texas.

Someone knocks on the door.

"Hey," I say. "I can call my cousin again. She can probably come and get me—I'd really like to get to her place, you know? It's like you said. It's been a long day."

The detective nods as he rises and walks to the door. It cracks open; a face fills it. They stand inches apart, talking in murmurs, but I hear snippets.

"...detective on a plane..."

"...he's coming out here?"

I hear one word out of the next sentence: "Tattoo."

The confidence that drove me earlier melts, pools in my shoes and overruns them, spreads out across the floor in a puddle the color of my soul.

They can only be talking about one man. It can only be Detective Alvarado. If he sees me, everything ends.

"Hey, Ryan, let me get back to you on that, okay? I need to check on something."

And with that, Charlie leaves me alone in the room. Right now, being Sean Reilly again doesn't seem so appealing.

36. Grandfather

THE SECOND HAND TICKS ON, guided by the nest of gears behind it, wheels turning in unison. The mechanics of the clock stretch unseen, connecting itself by thin axle to my fate. Each time metalwork clicks into place, Detective Alvarado is drawn closer to this room. The timekeeper is plotting against me, pushing myself and the man who hunts me together with every swoop of the pendulum.

Two hours. I sit in the conference room for two hours, head down, counting my breath. I do not sleep for a moment.

Jack and I are connected in this, resting on opposite ends of the same cog. Even though I can't talk to him, everything I've told the detective will filter through. I only hope he sees my lack of information as the peace flag I mean it to be.

Who knows what he will do, if Alvarado gets here. That tattoo, that damn tattoo—I told them about it, and now it marked Jack for death. What a stupid thing for him to put on his body, a stupid defiance.

The door to the conference room opens; I peel my face from my arms, wipe the spit from my lip, and turn to face Detective Green.

"Sorry about the delay," he says. "There's a lot going on today. Heck, there always is."

"It's no problem," I answer, though every cell of my being aches to escape this place. "Do you really need me to stay here this whole time? My leg really hurts. I want to go to my cousin's. I can come back and answer questions tomorrow, if you want."

Tomorrow, when I'm across state lines. Hopefully.

"I'm going to want to talk to her, too," the detective says.

Like I suspected. Pleasant, but still plotting my downfall.

I know this can't happen, but I don't know how else to answer, and so only nod. "Let me give her a call. You still have my phone, though."

Charlie holds out a hand, nods, and digs into the pocket of his slacks. My phone emerges, black plastic clamshell. He flips it open, mashes a few buttons.

"Go to my call history," I tell him, when it becomes clear he'll be the one operating the phone.

He does so.

"It's the first number there, that's her." I direct him to the number for Morgan's disposable cell phone.

"And what's her name?" he asks.

"Cassandra," I repeat, knowing that Morgan hasn't heard this name, and may spoil the entire charade within five seconds of answering the phone. She doesn't know she's supposed to be my cousin, or that she supposedly sent her boyfriend to retrieve me from Orlando.

He presses the speakerphone button. After the third ring, someone answers.

"Hello? Her voice is thin and compressed over the little speaker.

Charlie and I make eye contact, and I seize the opportunity to get the first word in. "Cassandra?" I ask. "This is Ryan White, I'm looking for my cousin Cassandra. I'm at the police station."

"This is her roommate, Sarah," Morgan answers back, without missing a beat. "Do you need someone to pick you up?"

The detective speaks up: "Sarah, you're on speakerphone. This is Detective Green, with the Ocala police department. We're very interested in talking with your roommate, do you know when she'll be back?"

"You know, it's strange, she's supposed to be here—come to think of it, I didn't see her this morning." Morgan's voice is upbeat and cheerful, each phrase given a pitch and timbre to vary it from the last.

"Is it okay if I stay at her house, like we planned?" I ask the phone. "I really need a place to stay tonight."

"Of course," Morgan says. "Your room is all set up. I can be there in ten minutes, is that okay?"

"That'll be fine," Detective Green says.

For a second, I really do love Morgan.

"Okay guys, hold tight, I will be there in a minute."

The detective pressures me for more information while we wait, but I dance around every comment, give him nothing to verify. Within fifteen minutes, a woman pokes her head into the conference room and tells us Sarah is here.

"You have my number," I tell him. "I will come up here tomorrow if you need me. I'm not going anywhere." I give my cast a good-natured knock.

Charlie runs a hand over his mouth, sighs. He starts to say something, then stops himself.

Have I gnawed through my tether?

Moments pass. He still hasn't said I can go.

If I could run out, I might. The clock is ticking, drawing Alvarado near. So I rise to my feet, crutches in hand. "My leg is killing me," I point out. "I really want to go lay down."

Charlie rises slowly. "Let me lead you out front. I'd like to have a word with Sarah."

The larger man opens the conference room door for me, and I hobble out, then turn and wait for him. We make our way through the dingy office building, with its water-stained ceiling panels and worn carpets. We pass a Hispanic teenager in handcuffs and two women having a heated argument. A thin, nearly toothless man lays back against a wall, open mouthed and snoring.

Then we're on the front steps, and Morgan is resting in the back seat of a taxi. When she sees me, she rises.

Big, perky smile. Not the Morgan I know—but then, it shouldn't be.

"What kind of trouble did he get into?" she asks as she approaches.

"Wrong place at the wrong time," the detective says, shaking Morgan's hand. "Look, we've got your roommate's boyfriend locked up, and what I believe is your car impounded. Did you lend it to anyone today?"

Morgan pauses, shakes her head. "Yeah, I let Skelton drive it to pick up Ryan, here."

"There was a dead body in the trunk," Charlie says simply.

She presses a hand to her open mouth, gasping. "What are you saying?"

"Cassandra's boyfriend was driving, Ryan here was in the back seat. There was a body in the trunk, naked, in a bag, been dead a while. Could be from a graveyard, or a morgue or something. Could you tell me a little bit about Cassandra's boyfriend?"

"You mean Skelton?" she asks.

"Skelton?"

"You know, like a skeleton. Because he's skinny, white and bald. That's him, right?" Morgan asks.

Everything, a manipulation.

"Do you know his real name?" he asks, one hand shuffling the keys in his pocket.

I turn, watch up and down the street. A white sedan is pulling up behind Morgan's taxi, the kind of nondescript American car no one actually buys. Possibly a rental.

Morgan appears to wrack her brain, finger to lips, brow clenched in concentration.

"Hank, Mike, Steve, maybe? Something basic like that. I don't know. Everybody calls him 'Skelton,'" she says. "He's kind of a loser, if you ask me. And believe me, I've told Cassandra before. She always wants to date someone she can fix." Morgan critiques the person we've both invented over the past few hours, making her that much more real.

I reach for Morgan's skirt and tug gently. Two men are getting out of freshly arrived car—a heavyset white man, and a Mexican with salt-and-pepper hair.

Detective Green extends a hand with a business card. "Let Cassandra know it's critical she gets in touch with us," he informs.

"Will do," Morgan says, taking the card and smiling. "And when can I get my car back?"

He shrugs helplessly. "Call back tomorrow, they'll have more information."

Morgan curses under her breath and smiles simultaneously. Then, she turns to the taxi.

Sweet mercy, finally.

The two men who arrived moments after Morgan are approaching—we're going to walk past each other on the narrow sidewalk. I keep my eyes focused on the ground between my crutches, head down. Out of my peripheral, I watch them pass.

One of the two men has acne scars across his face in deep pits. This man is Detective Alvarado.

He passes by. There is nothing between us but a cheap bottle of blond dye and some blue contacts. I propel myself as quickly as I can toward the taxi, throwing my crutches on the floor of the back seat. I force my bad leg in, trading the pain for a bit of speed.

Morgan's inside with me, running her fingers through her hair to tame a rogue lock.

"Go," I whisper. "Go, just go."

"Nearest hotel, please," Morgan says to the driver, still cheerful.

Our doors slam shut. The taxi driver, a dark-skinned man with black hair combed to the side, only nods as he puts the car in gear.

I twist and stare back at the police station. Detective Alvarado turns, and he's staring at my face in the window, mouth open.

"Go. He sees me, just go."

We creep away, driver taking every precaution in front of the police station. As we do, Alvarado points at us, and begins half jogging toward the taxi. He's saying something to Detective Green, and though I can't hear it, I can guess.

The words are my personal armageddon—everything I've done since I jumped off the bridge was to avoid this. Alvarado is telling a police officer that Sean Reilly is alive, and he's running.

37. Run

"**H**E SAW ME," I whisper, turning until my mouth is near her neck. "That's the detective from Port Lavaca—he saw me. He's coming."

Morgan doesn't give any sign she's heard me. Instead, she leans forward and presses her hand to the cab driver's shoulder. "I want to go to the historic district."

The driver nods.

I watch her for answers. She squeezes my hand and stares ahead. Face fixed in a smile, but eyes telling a different story—tight, focused.

The taxi turns to Ocala's main street, a thirty mile-an-hour quagmire with stoplights on every corner. Shops line the road, but not real stores. Not things people actually need. Bridal boutiques and wine bars, all upscale southern charm. Evening is still hours off, and the sun beats in full force—pedestrians stay clear, and the streets are mostly deserted.

Something shifts the crutches at my feet. Morgan reaches for a familiar black duffel bag, which she lifts this into her lap, hugging it to her body.

She touches her hand, then points out my window. When I look at her, she nods slowly. I feel like I'm supposed to know what this means, but I don't. Still, I wrap my good foot under the crutches, ready to move.

She presses her palm to the driver's shoulder again. This time, money is between her fingers, little green packet of prestige.

"Stop right here, please. Just pull over and stop, thank you."

Moments pass painfully before he notices the money in his peripheral, then takes it. He counts four fifties, spends another split second to process that data, and pulls into the right lane. Our stop is sudden.

Morgan's door is open before he's fully parked—she climbs out, bag in hand. I struggle to open my door and grab the crutches, and am left making uncomfortable eye contact with the driver as I finally pull myself upright and move.

She's waving at me from across the street, where she stands in front of a rectangular bus—a red city tour, ancient faces peering out the windows. I shuffle to her as traffic on either side of the road stops at the sight of a crippled guy.

Then we're on the bus, my crutches slick on the metal panels of the steps. Morgan's smiling, thanking the bus driver for her patience, and handing over a ten dollar bill. Keep the change.

I'm lowering myself into my seat as the bus kicks into motion, and the movement pushes me back into the hard plastic. I wince as my knee is strained, but land beside Morgan, whose leg is pressed to mine.

She grabs my hand and pulls—I turn to her, and she's staring out the window.

Three police cruisers turn the corner, and lights start flashing. By the time we've pulled past the traffic light, our cab from moments ago is swarmed—one car in front, behind, and beside it. Doors open and officers emerge with guns drawn.

The first real sign of what I've brought upon myself. The manhunt. I've defied authority, given the finger to the State and everything it stands for. Now, it's retribution. Now, this nigh omnipotent fraternity will do what it always does when it's threatened: obliterate the problem. Teach the lesson.

"You're going to get me killed," Morgan says, eyes forward. My hand is still in hers.

"What did I do wrong?" My voice twists on itself; sounds more like I'm whining than I mean to.

She turns to me, blue satellites trained on my pupils. "You didn't do anything wrong, Sean. This is Mr. Banks' fault. No one should have been driving bodies around after the week we've had. But, you're going to need to keep up. You don't exactly blend in with those things." Morgan nods at my crutches and cast.

Something within me sinks, disappointed. There's no good response, so I turn to stare out the windows of the bus.

Morgan withdraws her hand from mine. "I don't mean to make you feel bad. Look, we're really in it right now. This is a manhunt; they're going to set a perimeter and check everyone in it."

"We need to get out of here."

"Here, yes. But we can't leave the city until tomorrow morning."

"That's crazy." I face her, stare at her cheek.

"Cole's body is in the morgue, burnt to shit. I need to be there tomorrow to pretend to be his daughter and sign the cremation papers, while they still think he's the trailer's owner."

"How important can that be?"

Morgan speaks, voice still low and controlled, eyes forward. "If they suspect foul play, they'll look at the body. They'll see the bruises, the ether in his blood. May even figure out he's a dead sheriff. That happens, they'll start unraveling everything. They'll find me, and they'll find Ethan, take him out of the home I made for him. The only way to stop that from happening is to cremate him. The science is too good, otherwise. Can't leave them something to work with."

"Ethan?"

She says nothing, and doesn't need to. The question escaped my mouth before I thought it through. Her son.

38. Dragged

MORGAN CLUTCHES MY ARM. "This one. Get ready."
I pick up the crutches, holding one in each hand.

She rises first, walking down the center aisle, past the other two people on the bus. I follow, crab-like, crutches out to the sides. My shoe hits the cement. More one-story brick businesses, art galleries and music stores.

I struggle to keep pace with Morgan. Each stride with the crutches launches me forward, foot coming off the ground in long leaps. I follow her to the end of the block and make a right turn. The moment I round the corner, she pulls me to the side of the building.

A police cruiser drives up the street we turned from, and stops. His flashing lights reflect off the 'No Parking' sign a few feet from our hiding place.

Morgan tugs me forward. We cross another bus stop before I turn and look: the police are surrounding the bus that brought us here. One tendril of the great force that hunts us.

My guide beckons; I'm led into the vestibule of a small café. I barely catch the door as she steps inside. We're met by the rich smell of roasted coffee beans. Pastries line a glass case; I'm starving, and my stomach screams for them.

One middle-aged woman is camped out at a table in the corner—laptop, charger, phone, notebook, headphones, and coffee. Otherwise, the place is deserted.

Morgan walks to the barista. "Could you call me a cab?" she asks. "I spilled coffee all over this blue shirt, I need to go home and change." She motions at an imaginary stain on her blue blouse.

"You mean, like now?" the woman behind the counter sounds suspicious.

"Yes, please. Tell them it's for Sarah and Sean, we'll meet them right out front." Morgan reaches across the counter, hand extended, dollars offered. "For your trouble," she says as the barista takes the money from her hand.

I follow her back outside. We turn to the right, and continue down the sidewalk a few yards until she pulls me right again. "Create doubt," she tells me. "Sow confusion."

I say nothing, only follow Morgan into a clothing store—a southern chain, filled with local brands. Fake bling everything; sequins and glitter, fifty shades of pink. Aging store, rectangular ceiling panels stained and sagging.

One clerk oversees the entire shop, and sits at a great counter in its center. As we move through, Morgan picks clothes off the rack without stopping to check prices or sizes. We walk straight to the dressing room, and I take the stall next to hers.

She throws a pair of gray sweatpants and a blue shirt over the wall. "Put these on," she whispers.

I do as she says unquestioningly, stripping my shorts down over my cast.

"They're searching for us, but even more than that, they're looking for a boy with crutches, a woman in a blue blouse, black skirt. That's all 'Sarah' and 'Sean' mean, now."

The sweats are four inches too wide at the waist, but as I pull them over my legs, I see this wasn't a mistake. It's to accommodate the black plastic cast, to hide my most distinguishing feature. A drawstring ensures they won't fall off while I run.

"I'm not Sean Reilly," I mumble.

"Not what you said a week ago," Morgan calls from her stall.

As I tie my shoes, I realize she's right. I'm running as hard as I can from being Sean Reilly. Whatever I felt earlier about being unsure who I am, I'm not acting like I want to be him again. My best chance was there in the police station, with Charlie, and I didn't take it.

Sean Reilly is a bit of a lost cause, at this point.

I'm never getting that name back. Not unless the police catch me and force it on me. First time I've admitted it.

Morgan beats me out of the dressing room; she's wearing a floral sundress, and large tortoiseshell sunglasses mask her face. I follow her to the front, crutches pushing me along. She hands a wad of bills to the cashier. "Keep the change," I hear her say. "We're in a rush."

As we make for the exit, Morgan snatches a stylish straw hat from a mannequin. It's bound with a pale blue ribbon, and Morgan folds her hair up with one hand before situating the hat on her head.

She stops at the door, and I bump into her outstretched hand. A police cruiser creeps by, slowly.

"Give me those," she says, voice taut, nodding at the crutches.

"I need them to get around," I say without thinking.

"Just leave them here, now," she whispers. "Lean them up against the door. You can spot them a mile away."

"I won't be able to walk!" I'm panicking, now.

Morgan glares.

Every iota of me screams not to, but I bundle the crutches in one hand and set them by the door. I balance on one leg, shrugging helplessly, glaring.

She puts one arm around me and pushes open the glass door. I lean into her and hop on one foot, moving cautiously, and almost fall when she moves a step too far ahead.

"This doesn't look conspicuous at all," I say, dripping sarcasm. She barely manages to balance us both when we start to fall.

Morgan sighs and stops. We stand, clutching each other on the sidewalk. A party supply store to our right, a trophy shop across the street.

"Stand behind this," she says, pointing at a thick brick pillar that supports the cement awning overhead. It blocks me from prying eyes on the street. "Act like your leg isn't broken. I'll be back in a minute."

"Where are you going?" I ask.

"To buy that car," she says, nodding at an aging blue sedan in a nearby parking space. A 'For Sale' sign sits in the window, black paint and orange lettering faded from months in the sun.

I watch as Morgan steps into the party supply store next door, duffel bag over her shoulder, and hear her inquiring loudly about the car. Her voice is innocent, friendly, all smiles. Morgan *bubbles*. Never heard her bubble before.

Moments later she exits, then walks to the florist next door. Now she's gone for a bit longer, and I'm stuck on lookout, knowing I couldn't run anyway.

Hiding from my own name. Never thought it would come to this.

When Morgan returns, she's trailed by a middle-aged woman with hair cropped to a short bob around her face, necklace made from seashells and glitter.

"Are you sure you don't want the spare key?" she asks.

"I'll pick it up tomorrow, when I get the title," Morgan says. She's zipping the duffel bag closed.

"And this number is how I get a hold of you? In case something goes wrong?"

"What can go wrong? I paid you in cash." Morgan isn't looking at the woman, and instead focuses on pressing her new key into the car door. It unlocks.

I rotate myself with a hop, leaning sideways against the pillar and watching the exchange. Morgan motions me to come along, and so I do, bouncing carefully off the sidewalk, putting my hand on the hot hood of the car for balance. The paint fades at the edges, rust-ridden.

Before I get inside, the woman tucks into my door and pulls the glove box open, grabbing an armload of documents and dusty chargers.

"We really are in a rush," Morgan says sweetly. "Remember, I'm going to stop by tomorrow so we can work all this out. I just need to get him to practice. Like I said, my husband owns a scrap yard, so it's still a very good buy for me."

"And this is...?" she asks, turning to me, extending a hand, all smiles and excitement. Can feel every bone in her limp hand.

"That's my little brother," Morgan answers.

I smile, then let go. Before she can start another sentence, I hop inside, supporting my weight with my hands on the door and seat.

Morgan starts the car. It sputters to life: weak, tired thing.

"Good call," I say.

"When I pull behind this building, you're going to get out of your seat and jump in the trunk. Fast as you can. Got it?"

I'm learning to hate trunks.

She pulls into a shopping center then drives past the parking lot, to the side of the long, rectangular building and behind it. Once we're a few yards out of sight, where the employees smoke cigarettes and the trash cans brim with cardboard boxes, she slams the brakes. She's at my door by the time I open it.

Morgan pulls me up out of the car; I wrap an arm around her, and the breeze blows the few strands of hair that escaped her hat into my face.

We move to the trunk; the key turns, resulting in a metallic *clunk*. The little blue coffin lid lifts, opening to a small, cluttered space. Can't fit in here.

A cardboard box full of torn paperbacks. A package of plastic forks. An empty fast food bag—each is tossed on the ground. We dump this poor woman's little pile of personal clutter on the cement; books flutter in the wind, pages flipping on their own accord. Some blow free and press against the side of the shopping center.

In moments, I'm pressing my back to the bottom of the trunk, wedging my shoulders between the worn fabric and the raw steel of the lid. I can feel the outline of a spare tire under me, the ridge where the base bulges around its hub.

Morgan throws in the duffel bag, and closes out the sun.

39. As I stood across the gulf

"**Y**OU OKAY IN THERE?"

Her voice comes from everywhere and nowhere, reverberating through the steel shell of the car.

"Can you hear me?" I ask.

"Yeah, I hear you. I asked if you're okay."

I feel us slow down as we cross a speed bump. "Not my favorite place, if I'm honest. But, I'm okay. I mean, if it gets us out of here." I shout to be heard, and my own voice rings in my ears.

"Can't promise that," Morgan says. "Just one step at a time."

The gear shifts, changes the timbre of the motor.

"You think we'll make it?"

"If we can lose this car and get a new one in the next half hour, maybe. If you stay hidden, maybe. Maybe, Sean. I'll see the coroner first thing in the morning, minute he opens. I sign two forms, he witnesses it, and I'm done. Then we can go north, get out of Florida. Maybe spend a few years in Canada. I'll get a tan, dye my hair, and change identities. It's fine."

She doesn't sound like it's fine.

"Have you ever done something like this before?"

It takes her a moment to answer. "No, Sean. I haven't. I spent my whole life avoiding something like this."

The car lurches to a stop, brake metal grating on the wheels. "Are we stopping because we're getting pulled over?" I ask.

"No, Sean. I'll let you know before we go to jail. This is a red light."

"Thanks, Morgan."

Feels like hours before we stop, and the trunk opens. When it does, I lean out and see only towering weeds. Ferns so tall they climb over the car, and there's nothing but a fading greenish yellow in every direction.

"It'll only be a minute," Morgan says. The duffel bag is open on my lap, and she's digging through it.

The gun comes out first. This goes into her purse, followed by a stack of hundred dollar bills.

"You sure you're going to be okay?" I ask, ducking low to keep from banging my head on the trunk's lid.

"What would you do if I wasn't?" Morgan asks, sliding open the cylinder of the pistol, checking inside, then sliding it shut.

I don't have an answer for that.

"Guard the money," she says. "Get your gun. You might as well keep it on you, we're down to that."

"And what am I supposed to do with it?"

"Kill yourself. Kill someone, I don't know. That about covers what the gun can do for you."

I dig into the duffel bag and find the snubnosed thirty-eight. I don't even touch it, just watch where it sank between two stacks of cash.

"Morgan, wait."

Her arm is already gone to the green, broken into the thick ferns that shield us.

"I want to know something."

She stops, turns, withdraws her arm. Fingertips fall back into the light.

"What do you want to know, Sean?" she asks, voice polite, but strained. Her talents on display, a controlled calm.

"Tell me what happened with Kayla." My hand isn't exactly on the gun, just in the bag with the pistol, but I'm not moving.

"What about Kayla?" she asks.

"Stop trying to narrow down the question. Just tell me your role in her death." I swallow hard. "Please. I want to know, in case we get caught soon. In case I don't see you again."

"Okay, Sean. We're all very nervous now, it's a trying time. I'll tell you what happened. Can I step over here?"

And then I realize Morgan is talking to me like I'm about to shoot her, and she's moving like she wants to get closer to the gun.

I don't want her to think those things. Still, though—what will it take to get a straight answer?

"You can stand wherever you want."

She nods, taking one step to the side. Her hands are folded at her waist, and Morgan stands prim.

"Did you help murder Kayla?" I ask.

"Before Cole, I never murdered anyone—I guess we're all going through changes. Kayla was going to be our newcomer, someone to take my place so I could take Jack's. We wanted someone young, someone who could play a daughter. Less suspicion that way."

She swallows, then continues: "The morning Kayla died, I was in the car. Jack was about fifty yards away, on the beach, waiting to meet Kayla. We were both about two miles north of you, on the opposite side of the causeway."

While I stood and watched her fade into the gulf.

"I sat there for a while, maybe thirty minutes. Then Jack came up to the car, and uh..." She swallows. "And his hands were bleeding, where he'd cut himself while he stabbed her. Jack was freaked, just standing there and bleeding, staring at nothing. I was pissed, I didn't know why he did it. We went to Kayla's body—it was laying on the shore, half in the water." Her voice is tight, tired. "Jack couldn't lift her on his own, so I helped. We found some rope, tied Kayla to a broken cinder block, tried to keep her from coming up. Burial at sea. There was no time, you know, at six thirty in the morning. The spot was secluded, but someone would come by eventually."

I glance down; a spider crawls from a brown shrub to reach my sneaker. I kick it away. "So if you two were picking her up—when you told me about the 'getaway car' and drove me around, that was all a lie? You just showed me an empty space and told me her car was gone?"

"What did you expect? I just met you."

And she tricked me so easily. I really thought Kayla might be alive, for a minute. Until I blinked, and the police tore my world apart.

She continues: "I wanted to get you away from Jack while I could. The minute you showed up, I knew it was over. No one ever told me you knew Kayla faked her death. You turned everything upside down. I distracted you, and Jack cleaned up the house and ran. And now this, which I can honestly say is the craziest thing I've done yet. I like to stay months ahead of the police, and now it's minutes."

I look up from my feet. "How do I know that's all true?"

All I catch is her silhouette as it's devoured by the scenery. "You don't."

40. Fingerprint

"**S**EAN!"

Night has fallen by the time I hear her voice again. I wake up with a start, banging my head on the trunk. I lift a hand to rub the pain away, and realize I'm holding the pistol.

"Where are you?" I call.

"I can't find you, just follow my voice."

I heft myself out of the trunk, then land on my good leg. The duffel bag comes with me, strapped across my chest. The gun goes into my pocket, so that I can press both hands into the weeds below, and push myself forward.

I crawl through the track left by one of the wheels, walled in by tall grass. Crickets dive-bomb, some knocking against my face and arms, others buzzing off into the thicket.

I press into the soft surface of an ant pile; I curse, withdraw the hand and shake it violently, skittering past before I'm swarmed with angry insects.

Then I'm clear, and there's a thin black road in front of me. I hear the lumbering motor of a large diesel, and turn to see Morgan sitting behind the wheel of an old Chevy truck.

I look back—the tall grass consumes any trace of the car, proud sprouts jutting up. With one hand on the truck, I hop around to the passenger side and pull open the door. The steel button resists at first, then depresses reluctantly when I push harder. The seat is one long bench, fake leather slippery under my sweatpants.

When I'm in, she takes off.

Morgan seems to absorb starlight, moonskin glowing pale. I watch as she drives, both hands on the thin, hard steering wheel, forehead tensed in concentration. The road ahead is barely lit by the aging headlights.

We drive down a small country highway, a narrow road split by faded yellow lines, reflectors chipped and missing. After a time, she slows near a brick sign that stands guard outside a simple brown building. *Ocala County Medical Examiner's Office.*

The building sits in an open field in front of someone's unkempt, wild grassland. Morgan drives past, turns right. Another narrow road, this one lacking lines to mark lanes, leads us a few hundred yards behind the office.

"Think we can make it?" she asks, nodding at a wall of plants off to the right. They stand in a tight-packed row like soldiers in formation.

"You mean, can we drive through that? Why would you want to?"

She pulls off the road, heading directly into a patch of ferns, wheels dipping into mud then sucking out with a slurching sound. Morgan curses under her breath when a tire spins uselessly, but in moments we're free. The truck crashes through the walls of green, plants scraping the undercarriage. When I turn to look back, I see nothing but tall weeds.

She turns off the truck. The lights dim, the sound of the engine dies, and all that's left is silence.

"This is it," she says, rolling down her window, thin arm cranking the manual control.

"This is what?" I ask.

"This is where we're sleeping tonight. Come on, I got a truck for a reason." She opens her door, pushing it open with her foot as the wall of flora resists. I do the same, and soon my good leg is pressed into the soft greenery of the wild field.

We meet at the tailgate, which she lowers. I pull myself up, then slide back over the uneven metal bed of the pickup.

I sit in the corner of the platform, with my back pressed to the cabin, knee against the wheel well. Morgan climbs in, rising fully then walking to me. She lowers herself down.

Didn't know she'd want to sit so close. Morgan's legs are pressed to mine, and her arm slides behind my torso. She keeps coming. Brown hair presses against my chest; I can feel the warmth of her cheek. My arm rises instinctively, wraps around her shoulders, pulling her closer.

She's doing it again.

I direct my eyes at the night sky. Coruscant brilliance; the stars are out in force, fistful of gems flung into the void.

Morgan's hand rises to rest on my chest, fingers curling against my shirt. The scent of her thins my blood, makes it electric and wild in my veins. My whole being responds to her nearness, some switch flicked within me.

I wonder what's triggered this latest display. Maybe she feels sorry for me—maybe she knows we're doomed. Like this is an apology for everything having gone to hell.

Or, maybe I got too close when I asked for the truth about Kayla. Maybe this is another way to keep me on the leash.

As I learned, though, 'why' matters least. I can try to pick apart her motivations, unmake and remake her with my mind, but it will never matter. She will do what she wants, and I will let her.

I want it, and she knows.

The closeness makes Morgan much more real. She's small, thin, and fragile. Easy to forget I'm larger than her, easy to forget she's human.

I begin to count my breath, hoping to calm down, but the numbers leave me. The oxygen is rarefied, burns in my lungs.

All this riotous sensation guides itself to one act: I tighten my grip on Morgan's shoulder and pull her closer to my chest. I lower my lips to her forehead and kiss it softly.

Her eyes turn to mine. "You okay?" She's smiling. Her elbow, which rests on my torso, dips downward and rubs against the solid bulge in my sweatpants.

Red heat fills my cheeks. I try to talk, to say something, to apologize, but only stutter out nonsense.

Her hand spreads open across my chest, then trails lower. My skin throbs; I can feel the ridges of her fingerprints as they drag across my flesh. Every nerve ignites.

The fingers slide lower, pushing back the band of the wool pants, exposing me. I stare upwards; the stars seem to be spinning gently.

Morgan's hand wraps around me, soothing, a nurse rehabilitating an injured patient. She is rhythmic, soft, and methodical as she tames me. I breathe a ragged gasp, toes curling—knee hurting—then working to relax, can't tense that leg, the sensation of her cool hand driving me rabid. My fingers clutch her shoulder. The other hand presses against the pitted metal of the truck, drags across it, rust flaking off against my skin.

The moments pass indeterminably. In minutes, or seconds—I don't know—my awareness flares from the little gem at my center to a raging havoc, consuming me. As these spasms gradually subside, a calm hollow takes its place. Morgan withdraws her hand, laughing gently.

"Better?" she asks.

"Better," I answer, sighing heavily.

41. Mud

BY THE TIME I AWAKE, my leg is hot in the advancing dawn. The sun rises over the front of truck, climbing my body as it pulls back the shade of the cabin.

Morgan is gone. I twist, searching, and find her sitting in the front seat, staring into the rearview mirror. Her purse is open and she's applying eyeliner. A brush and lipstick rest on the dash.

I pull myself up, hands on the metal under me and then the roof. My cast aches against my skin, pressed nearly to my bone as I slept. I move my thigh from side to side, trying to ignore the tingling numbness as feeling returns to my leg.

My knee is sore from the day of ducking and hiding, hips and shins bruised where the cast grinds against me. I'd give anything to be able to run. Seems like that may come in handy.

"Get up on the roof of the truck," Morgan says, voice muffled through the glass between us.

I do so, hoisting myself up until my legs are draped across the rear window.

"Okay, look straight ahead, the direction the truck is facing."

I turn, following her instructions, shielding my eyes with an open hand. I'm perched over the overgrown field of tall weeds and the skeletal cypress trees they choke.

The back of the medical examiner's office is only a hundred yards away. A chain link fence with a barbed wire crown guards a metal shed.

"You see the morgue?"

"Yeah," I answer. "I see it."

She says nothing—I decide to fill the void.

"Hey, let me ask: Is it all worth it?"

I can feel her voice through the roof of the truck. "What?"

"This, everything. Being a fugitive."

"Given my options, yeah."

"What about Mr. Banks? You said it yourself, it's his fault we got pulled over. Now you're cremating a body to keep yourself out of prison. How can anything be worth that?"

"I'm cremating my ex-husband so I'm not in your shoes a week from now," she says dryly. "But, Mr. Banks can keep you safe. He really can. He can also get you killed, but he can keep you safe. Not many people on this earth can say that to someone like you, someone the whole world is searching for. He can keep you safe, and he can make you rich. Come down here."

As I climb down, Morgan keeps talking: "You're going to drive me around to the examiner's office, then drop me off and come back here. When I'm done, I'll signal you from the back of the building, where you're looking now. Then, come around and pick me up, and we'll get the hell out of Florida."

She slides over, and I climb into the driver's side of the car. Thankfully, it's an automatic, and I can drive with one leg.

The truck lurches, climbing easily over ground that sucked at our tires only yesterday, wheels pulling us over the broad-leaf ferns we flattened on our trip out.

I stop at the edge of the street, good foot pressing down the brake, which does nothing until the pedal is flush with the body of the car, then stops all at once. The dashboard clock says eight in the morning, and the farm road is quiet.

We turn twice, and I stop in front of the stone sign marking the medical examiner's office. Morgan hops out, same sundress, makeup pristine, with her inconsolably tangled hair hidden under the straw hat. She pulls a mailing envelope from the duffel bag, then sets the bag and her purse in the floor of the truck. Then she shuts her door, and is gone.

I don't like this. Still, I drive on, alone.

On the return trip, I pass a policeman, going the opposite direction. My first instinct is to speed up, or turn and run—but I repress those urges. I stare straight ahead, tell myself repeatedly that there's nothing to fear. Make it true.

The cop passes. Nothing happens.

I return to our trail into the tall weeds, making sure no one is around before I pull in. I do what I've been told, and park in the same flattened clearing. After I kill the engine, I climb up into the trunk, then on the roof.

The sun breaks past a haze of morning clouds, and the metal warms from it. Just getting started, though—by midday, it will be twenty degrees hotter.

I wait and worry. Another cop car rolls down the street where the coroner's office rests. Could be routine, or something that has nothing to do with us, or part of the manhunt. I don't like it. But, there is nothing else to do, and so I sit, and wait, and watch.

Less than an hour into my vigil, a figure turns the corner of the building and begins waving both arms into the air, in the direction of my truck. I cannot make out a face, but it must be her.

I jump into the bed, then down to the ground, pulling myself along, equal part hands and feet.

The truck awakens; I force the automatic transmission into reverse, lever reluctantly snapping into place with an extra shove of my arm. I crane my neck to see out the rear window as I back straight out, using the tracks I've already worn.

I miss the track. A wet *slurch*. My rear, driver's side tire slides down into a pit of mud; I accelerate instinctively, pressing on the gas. Mud flies, spat out of the wheel well—some lands with a plop on the side mirror.

Damnit. I press harder, but the truck only sinks further. I put it in park and jump out. I hop to the side, balancing against the vehicle. Wet muck swallows the bottom half of the wheel.

Morgan is waiting on me. I get back inside, try driving forward instead. I move a few inches—promising—but lose traction again and slip back.

I back up again, anxiety rising. We need this truck; we need to get out of Florida.

Reverse gets me nowhere. I hit the gas, twisting the wheel, climbing another inch before falling back. I repeat this, frantic now, turning the wheel left then right, in forward then reverse.

Minutes pass, but I refuse to give up. I roll down my window and lean halfway out to see what I'm backing into. Mud coats the rear windshield and side mirror, and I imagine I have dug a hole half the size of the ancient pickup.

Then, I manage to rock the truck out of the rut. When I reverse, the tire balances on the edge of the pit. My breath catches in my throat; I ease the wheel along, slowly reversing until I've edged around the ditch I dug.

I check the time on the dashboard: I've been trapped for twenty minutes. Sweat soaks my clothes, wets my hands. Can't get to the front of the medical examiner's office fast enough. The tires are mud slick and I slide a few inches into my turn, leaving wet dirt on the road in my wake. I turn the two corners to reach the coroner's office.

A crosswind strikes the car, sending grass clippings and dust through the open window and into the cabin. Some catches across my face; I begin blinking violently to clear my vision.

When I can see again, it's blue and red lights. They glow dimly in the sun; a police car is stopped at the side of the road, a few hundred yards away from the office and another few hundred more in front of me.

Shit. I drive past, staring out my window. The cruiser is empty. My eyes rise from the car to the grassland beyond: there he is, blue-uniformed back to me, trotting into the high grass. A few dozen feet in front of him, a woman in a floral sundress sprints full-speed through the weeds, outpacing the officer.

Morgan is running on foot. Damnit, she must have started walking when I didn't come. Maybe she was spotted by a passing cruiser.

I slow down; she's got him beat. The officer stops chasing, then lifts his radio to his chest. While barking instructions, he turns and sees me. I accelerate suddenly, driving past as Morgan disappears into the trees.

Just keep driving. Just keep driving.

How do I find her? I need to find her again.

I can't turn around, can't join the cop in the search for her. They'll see who I am, arrest me immediately.

Shit. Damnit, Sean, damnit, worthless truck and worthless mud. She needed me for one thing. Now what? She's running through the woods.

She might call. She has her—

I turn my head, look at the floor of the passenger seat. The black duffel bag rests, fat with money and guns. My knee holds the steering wheel in place as I bend down, grab the bag and bring it up next to me. I dig with a free hand.

I'm holding her phone. Morgan is gone.

42. Rock at the bottom

M Y MIND IS THE STILLNESS of bomb shattered eardrums. I spend an hour driving aimlessly, turning away from any major highways or residential areas. Thoughts move too fast, ideas jetting past, rebounding, colliding, fracturing into more, a television screen gone all static.

I must find Morgan. Conversely, I must also get the hell away. The two truths battle.

Blink, and chaos descends. How else could it be, when our enemies strike organized and without warning? The anxiety of it drives me mad. No wonder Morgan always seems in control—she knows at any moment she'll be tested, and freedom will be hers to win or lose.

Hope she wins.

Ultimately, fear and reason triumph. The police will be looking for Morgan. If I go near her now, they will find me, and I am the more wanted of the two of us. I can't seriously expect to just scoop her up. And I have the money; if she's in jail and I'm free, I can post bail.

It hurts me to do it—a tearing pain in my chest, like someone slammed a butcher knife on the link between us, severed it cold. But, I do. I abandon her.

Morgan is not the only one in trouble. I have the truck, the guns and the money—but she knows how to use them, and I don't. My best hope is to get clear of the manhunt.

I find a highway and drive west.

When I can, I'll check the news, find out if she's under arrest. If she isn't, I'll try to find her. If she is, then—I don't know. I don't know. That can't happen; Morgan is too smart, too careful.

Fleeing on foot, with a cop not twenty feet behind her. Some geniuses we are. All that rhetoric and posturing, and this is where we end up.

The interstate highway is busy, a steady flow of traffic. I insert the old diesel truck into a stream of newish sedans, feeling like a relic in a modern era. Time flows easy on the highway, and every mile between myself and Ocala makes me feel that much better.

Over an hour into my escape, I notice something. An electric message board blinks at the side of the road, broadcasting some public safety advisory. I watch it idly as I drive past, catching the flash of the blocky orange letters before I read the words.

Chevy Truck. Gray. License Plate DJK-5585. Armed and Dangerous, dial 9-1-1.

It must mean me.

My false sense of security shatters. Escaping Ocala means nothing; the whole state is after me. Maybe the nation. There isn't going to be any 'driving away.'

The world slows; I realize my foot has come off the gas.

This is it, then. There's no escape. Every car in eyesight might be calling the police right now. The roads are a trap and without them, I can't escape. It's checkmate.

I keep my foot off the gas, speed dropping to forty, thirty-five. A car swerves from behind, overtakes in the left lane.

It really was crazy to think this could work. Morgan can't even do it—I don't have a chance on my own. I can't even run, can't really even get out of the damn truck, since I don't have my crutches anymore.

It's time to give up, before I'm shot or something.

Or, maybe that's the answer. Being shot doesn't sound so bad, in the scheme of things. The real tragedy of death is everyone else's loss, and that's already taken care of. All that's left is pain, and who knows if it hurts to die like that. I mean, I bet it does, but for how long?

I'd never need to be Sean again. I might—maybe, I mean—I might rather die than go through it all.

The trial, the imprisonment, the attention. Being put in a cage and called by that name. Everyone lining up to see, to point, to force me to be a part of what they do. To mock me for trying to escape.

I have a gun here, right here in this bag. I could just end it.

I unzip the duffle bag, put my right hand inside and grip the pistol, as though to remind myself it's real.

And suddenly my death seems very close. Like a holiday coming later in the month, like an inevitability that will be here soon. Like I used to look forward to the weekend.

Really, no matter what, death is nearby. Either from suicide, or getting shot by the police, or maybe executed for murder.

But then, that's how it always is, isn't it? Everyone dies, they just don't think about it. It's not so different than the rest of my life, than the rest of everyone's life. Death is always there.

The moment this thought lights up my brain, something snaps within me. The chain breaks. A sort of mental shrug, a psychic sigh, and the depression I felt moments ago falls away.

It doesn't matter. I've already died, it's not that bad. It doesn't matter.

This is the bottom. Instead of the pit of despair I expected, there's some sort of peace. History is long, life is short, everyone dies. Small raft, big ocean, many sharks.

So, there's no problem with my continuing to run—there's nothing to lose. There's never anything to be afraid of, not ever.

It's as though I wore a harness my whole life, up until this moment, and I've just let it fall to the ground. It and everything I expected myself to carry.

Sean Reilly.

I've either broken my own mind, or broken through to something else.

My foot presses down on the accelerator. My speed climbs, elder engine bellowing out. I turn and look at a gray sedan in the lane next to me. A child in the rear seat stares back.

43. Getaway

T HE BLINKER CLICKS; I exit rolling past the burnt grass lining the ramp. I continue down the feeder for fifteen minutes, until I reach a small outcropping of gas stations and drive-through restaurants. A billboard with red lettering over a green camo backdrop points me toward something interesting; I turn right, following the posted directions.

Moments later, I arrive at an outdoor supply store and pull in. All the while, I check my rearview mirror for the police. None, yet, but I can't shake the feeling they are seconds away.

The supply store is a relic from the nineteen eighties, big brown cap on a squat rectangle of gray bricks. Trucks like mine litter the parking lot and two families with cardboard signs park near the road and sell puppies from a metal cage.

In front of the store rest a row of glittering red machines, tethered to the parking lot by steel cables. These are interesting.

I turn through the lot, driving to the far side of the building, where the employees park. I stop the car and push open the door.

I want to get rid of the license plates, because I figure it may buy a little time. I hop around to the front, hands scalding on the hood where I brace myself. With both hands on one edge of the plastic frame that holds the plate, I pull. The plastic is old and brittle; it snaps. Screws are torn from their place with tiny clouds of dust.

I repeat this in the rear of the truck, then throw the plates into the passenger side. My good leg aches, exhausted from pulling the weight of two.

Sun beams furious; I squint into it. Still got work to do.

I take the duffel bag, then hop to the side of the building, using it for balance. I maneuver to an abandoned shopping cart and lean on it, both elbows pressed into the grips, supporting myself as I slowly make my way to the front of the store.

Once there, an elderly man in a blue collared shirt greets me. I ask for a motorized cart; he looks surprised. I rap my knuckles across my cast. Through the sweatpants, the plastic rings hollow.

He returns with an electric red cart. I lower myself to the seat, black pleather already warm somehow, then pull my bad leg in with both hands. The duffel bag rests in my lap.

The greeter hovers nearby, and I realize I absolutely reek of sweat. My clothes are rank after two days on the run.

I smile at him.

I've got a couple million dollars—let's see what I can do with it. My thumb presses the accelerator, and I hum off down an aisle.

An hour later, I check out—cart overloaded, barely fitting between the aisles. Two aluminum trekking poles extend sideways, tungsten tips jutting from round shields. Under them, a folded up sleeping bag, and a hiking backpack full of camping supplies. Next to that, a gallon of water. A tag I missed on my new camouflage shirt pokes between myself and the seat.

I dip my hands in Morgan's duffel bag, peeling ten hundred dollar bills from the first stack I reach. I keep my hands low, out of sight, until I can bring the wad of money out and seal the bag once more. I'll pay her back.

The cashier guides my items across the scanner, gaze fixed blankly on his hands. I pay, and the reloaded cart hums along out of the store. The same elderly greeter offers to help load the bags into my truck; I refuse politely.

I ride the cart out of the building. It is excruciatingly slow, barely walking pace. My broken leg stretches out to the side, spreading me wide, like I'm lounging half-out of the ridiculous little buggy. The parking lot rolls under me, sunlight dazzling my eyes.

This very moment, probably a thousand police are organizing to capture me. They'll have helicopters, patrol cars, satellites, guns and radios. And here I am, humming along on a motorized shopping scooter. Must be the saddest fugitive there ever was.

A mad smile cracks my face.

I roll to the other end of the parking lot, next to an outdoor display of off-roaders. The little vehicles are distinctly insectoid, some mechanical arthropods in a half-dozen distinct species. They alternate red, black, and camouflage. Some sit high above their wheels with long angled headlights, all mantis and built for speed. Others crawl low on six wheels, with a deep, black metal tray gleaming along the rear.

A redheaded teenager in a blue uniform approaches—I have to remind myself we're the same age. "Hey. You looking to buy one of these?"

"Which one would get me furthest off road?"

44. Unlightenment

I TEST THREE, but settle on a sturdy, black beetle of a machine—flat rack in the back, and four fat, knobbed tires on the bottom. Of my options, this seemed the most rugged, the most able to handle the real wild, instead of some toy to speed around a field in.

I step down and pay for the all-terrain four-wheeler. Transaction complete, the teenage salesman returns with two wheel-width metal ramps under his arm. I stare.

"So you can load it into your truck," he explains.

"That's okay," I answer.

He cocks an eyebrow.

"I live right down the road," I say, nodding vaguely at the horizon. "I'll just get it down there."

"It ain't street legal," he warns me as he stuffs the receipt into the front pocket of my new backpack. "And don't you have a truck in the parking lot?"

"I'll be all right," I assure him. "Help me move my stuff over, would you?" I nod at the motorized shopping cart, three legged donkey to my new war horse.

The teenager lifts the bags and places them on the metal bars at the rear of my new ride; elastic straps are employed to tie everything down. The walking sticks stretch out dangerously, almost doubling the width of the machine. The salesman shrugs helplessly at this.

"You want that strapped down?" he asks, pointing at Morgan's black duffel bag, which I'm still wearing around one shoulder.

"No, thank you," I tell him, as the last strap is tightened and I climb on the machine. "I'll hold on to this one."

I twist the key, and the black Honda rumbles to life. The needle on the fuel gauge rises; it's nearly a full tank.

"That's your throttle and brake," the teenager says, pointing at the grip and accompanying lever. "And you shift gears right here."

Yellow buttons scored with plus and minus signs rest near the right handle. "Turn four-wheel drive on with this button."

I lift my broken leg with both hands, holding myself by the thigh, and work to push it into the footwell. It doesn't quite fit—the cast won't let me bend my knee, so the best I can do is leave my foot hanging from the edge.

"Maybe need to wait until you get that thing off," he says helpfully.

As though that's an option. "I'll be fine."

My hand finds the throttle and twists. I roll forward jerkily, hitting the gas too hard then releasing it in shock. I try again, rolling a few more feet across the parking lot.

I find my pace. With the press of a button, it shifts to second: the display reads 25 mph and rising. Hot wind shoots through my hair; I turn to the right, curving around the parking lot to my truck.

No stopping now. I fly past, toward the large, unkempt field behind the store. A line of trees fills the horizon.

No real plan. Just want to keep living until I have to die.

I quite like living. I like living with a bag of money and no name even more. But when I die, which could be soon, that'll be fine too. Just an end. Everyone has to end.

The wheels leave the parking lot and I bounce over the grass. I jump high over knotted ground; my broken leg is jarred as I crash down. The sensation goes right to the core of my nervous system, direct line to my spine. The pain hits deep and fades slow, leaving me gasping.

Just a little reminder I exist.

I slow down, climbing rather than flying over the humps. There is no evenness to the soil; it crests and dips like waves, and for a moment I think of Kayla's final journey into the gulf.

Seems like the gulf is all that's been consistent these past few weeks. The void where shadows are lost and ghosts emerge free.

My four-wheeler rolls slow; I can really only use the first two gears without hurting myself. The land is more forest than swamp, with only the occasional wet patch. When a wheel slips in the mud, my heart catches in my throat—but the all-terrain vehicle is ruthless, and a press of my four-wheel drive button always leads one of the fat, knobbed tires to grip solid ground, pulling me out.

This place makes it clear I'm an intruder. Most of my life has been spent in cultured environments—but this isn't tame, it isn't manicured. My presence is a violation, and the wild reacts.

A horde of tiny locust-like creatures skitter from a small bush as it scrapes the underside of the buggy, an explosion of buzzing black forms jetting in each direction. I shield my eyes with the crook of my arm and feel them knock against my legs.

When I bend back a tree branch to pass, a mockingbird chases me, furious as it flutters near enough that I can feel the pressure of its wings in my ears.

I soon watch for these dangers automatically, eyes constantly moving, always searching for the next threat, the next gleam of water that must be dodged. With my mind focused like this, the hours slip by unnoticed. Time doesn't matter—but what does matter is light, and the shade of the sky paints my experience. As the colors deepen, I know I'm further from my pursuers.

At times, I come to patches of impregnable thicket, or muddy pools whose depth are impossible to gauge. When I reach these obstacles, I turn, sometimes back-tracking for what feels too long, longer than it could possibly have taken to become trapped.

I don't know exactly where I'm going, except that when the option arises to pick a more cultivated landscaped, I don't take it. I drive deeper into the trees, into the wet. My only thought is to separate myself from civilization.

They have names, and labels, and crimes someone named Sean Reilly is responsible for. Things he didn't actually even do, which is beside the point. Ahead of me, though, in this raw Florida swamp, is a world that doesn't care about those labels. A place past names, for a nameless boy.

45. Aural

BY THE TIME NIGHT BEGINS TO FALL, it's been over an hour without a sign of anything modern. Only faded ruins: A gravel road half-sprouted with weeds, the remnants of a crude oil pump, the collapsed skeleton of a windmill. Once, I cross over a fallen chain-link fence. A metal plaque drilled to one of the fallen supports reads *Crystal River Nature Preserve.*

The four wheeler's glowing eye beams light across the wilderness. But as night falls, I lose the ability to scout the terrain far ahead. Three times, I find myself hopelessly lost among pools of water, unsure if I'm coming or going. It takes some panic, some thrashing around to find my entrance again and escape.

As the last traces of the sun vanish, I bring my little motor to a stop on a slight hill of hard dirt and thin grass.

Half a tank left. I keep the headlights on as I turn to inspect my gear, still tied to the rack.

When I was a kid, my dad used to take us out in our family sedan, to Gougane Barra—a nature reserve in Ireland. Our little car would roll along a gravel path far as it could, before we parked in a little lot and took our gear out of the trunk. He carried it all, big camping bag in one hand, tent strapped across his back, ice chest rolling along in the other.

That was barely camping, really—sleeping on a little plot of mowed grass, other families in shouting distance. We would lay there, stargaze and talk to each other. He was my father and I loved him.

The sadness is a tearing inside me. But it's past tense—I've accepted this. He is not dead, after all, and neither am I. We're just separated; I've been through the gulf. The son he knew is gone.

Still miss Dad, though. Strange, to think of him now. How can anyone ever say they're truly reborn, truly new? The memories travel with the ghost.

I draw one of the walking poles and press it against the soil. The tip digs in, but is stopped by the metal band, giving purchase. The grip isn't easy; it's almost vertical and strains my wrist. But, I can move. I manage a few shaky steps away from the four wheeler, sleeping bag under my free arm.

I shake out the man-sized sack. It's slim, light and cheap—I can't imagine it gets cold here in the Florida swamp. At least, I hope it doesn't. As I lay the bag across a short section of weeds, bugs leap away, buzzing into the distance.

They will be a problem. Insects fly out of the black like they're congealed pieces of it, little humming spots of darkness encroaching on my light. Mosquitoes congregate around me and moths knock against the ATV with dumb thumps.

After traveling back to the pack, I retrieve a flashlight, put the duffel bag over my shoulder and kill the headlight. The momentary blackness is all encompassing, and a little notch of panic constricts my neck while I fumble with the flashlight. Then, I find the switch. Sight, again.

I hold the light between my neck and shoulder, then find the sleeping bag and lower myself on it. The duffel bag goes down next to me.

Weeds form hard lumps and I can feel them through the thin cushion. I untie my shoes, then set them next to me. Slowly, I open my bag and crawl inside, bringing the flashlight, holding it close to my body.

One hand reaches out, feels for the duffel bag. I unzip it, removing the gun and setting it in the grass near my head. The safety is off. Still my last-ditch escape plan.

With it removed, I pull the two million dollar duffel bag in close, and rest my head on a thick pile of money. So much trouble over this little canvas sack and out here, it's reduced to my pillow.

It's not real sleep. It comes in fits and I'm jolted from it each time something crawls across or onto me. This brings frantic action as I sweep my hands across the smooth fabric, damp now with my sweat, and force a wriggling creature out.

Then I'm awoken by something worse: the deep chop of a helicopter as it floats past. I pull my head from the sleeping bag and peer up.

The predator passes slowly, low to the ground, distance from me impossible to judge. One mile, or ten. A focused beam of light aims downward, searching the earth.

The four wheeler sits in the open, a few feet away, threatening to expose me. But, there's no solution to that. There is nothing to do but wait and listen and hope.

The sound fades as it prowls on. I lie, tense, trying to pick the rhythmic hum of the helicopter's blades out from the chorus of crickets.

Nothing comes. I wait, now very awake, now past sleep. My adrenaline is drawn from newly discovered reserves, from this new core of myself I'm only discovering now.

My hand reaches along the grass, grabs the gun. It stays with me as I stretch out, prone, braced on my good leg and two arms.

I lie motionless for hours, watching, listening. The occasional beetle or centipede scuttles past and I knock it away with my fingers.

Then, something unexpected; so abrupt I jolt within the bag's confines, climbing up on my hands in surprise. It's not a helicopter, but it's not the wild, either. Something manufactured rings in my ears.

The duffel bag is chirping.

I listen for a few seconds before I realize what's happening. Doubly frantic now, I tear into the bag, searching with both hands through piles of money for the cell phone that's ringing.

It's in my hand; I press the answer button, praying it isn't too late.

"Who is this?" I ask.

"You know who." A woman's voice. Morgan.

"Holy shit, you're okay. Thank you, thank you, thank you. How did you get out?"

Her voice sends waves of relief through me. "I buried myself. Look, you need to save your battery. Where are you?"

"I don't know. I got a four wheeler, got off the road. I passed a sign that said 'Crystal River Nature Preserve.' I have your money," I say. "It's safe." In case she needed extra incentive to save me.

I hear the sound of fingers tapping on a keyboard.

"Do you think you can make it to the gulf?"

"The Gulf of Mexico?" I ask.

"Crystal River has a hundred channels, it looks like, and they all empty into the gulf. You get out there, stay on the beach. Listen, there is a smartphone in my bag. It might have some charge left. When you're ready, turn it on and I'll use it to find you. It may take me a while, so be visible."

"Give me a day or two, I'll find a way," I promise.

"Don't be late," she says.

"Don't give up on me," I tell her.

The line is dead. I return the phone to its place in the bag.

Violet fills the sky's edge, the barest peak of the sun's first blade slicing across the horizon. A deep blue follows, then a pinprick of orange, and I know it's time to move. I rise, gather the thin sleeping bag that's now heavy with sweat and dew, and roll it into a tight bundle. This is thrown at the four wheeler, and rolls to its wheel.

Hiking pole in hand, I stagger to the vehicle. My eyes adjust to the purple dim and I can make out the shapes of the taller weeds. Water glistens in small pockets between lumps of swamp.

The four wheeler rumbles to life. I turn on the headlight and within seconds, insects swarm to its glow, flying in helical structures through its warmth. I twist the accelerator and pull the little buggy out of the hole it dug for itself in the wet weeds, and slide slowly through the brush.

Some sort of forest looms ahead, and I want inside. Something in me knows—primal, beyond evidence—that the helicopter searches for me. If I'm spotted, there's nothing I can do. If I stay in the trees, though, maybe I won't be seen.

I got no real sleep. Nothing to eat, either. Just drive. Just a clear focus on each yard I gain, mind quiet, calm. Nothing distracts me, because for once, I am not distracted. Life is simple: I am, and I must be free.

What was it Mr. Banks asked me, when we first met? 'Did I like ghost stories?'

He knew, of course. Knew what I'd learn over time—that I am the ghost. That we all are, underneath everything else. Everything I destroyed, piece by piece.

46. A return to the water

I CLIMB OVER THICK ROOTS, angling for flat ground, never easing my focus. At times I brace against the four wheeler with my good leg, rising half out to balance as the ATV tilts, nose down, engine churning.

It takes until sunrise to reach the trees. Trunks stretch skyward, canopy of leaves forming a hundred foot high dome, this verdant bell enclosing me.

Except it's not a forest, like I hoped. A deep pool of water confronts me, surface silver, dotted with moss and unblossomed lilies. No puddle this time, but real water, deep enough to swallow the all-terrainer. It's not a forest at all; it's the heart of the swamp.

I watch the water. The surface is pristine, save the occasional ripple as fish break the barrier to snatch insects from their space on the plane. Dark roots curl from the muddy banks and into the water, thick pipes the antithesis of their cousins in Port Lavaca. Sucking water out, purifying, growing.

The air is wetter here and my clothes gather tiny droplets of moisture as I roll along. I travel at the edge of the water, keeping it on my right side to navigate. The shape of it can only be a river, but it seems to go nowhere in particular and has no order.

The path is interrupted by a wheel, tire rotting from its rusted rim, wedged between two roots. Next to it, a torn rag. A few signs of mankind, abandoned and worn.

I drive around, forced into a patch of thick mud that splashes on my shoes and jeans, coating my socks and cast.

By midday, I see a structure in the distance. It scares me, at first —I didn't imagine there'd be anything out here. All right angles and paint; shapes unknown to a swamp, things that don't belong. My wheels crunch along as I feather the throttle, creeping as best I can. It's the side of a cabin. A dirt road connects it to a few more.

I drive near the road, land leveling out as I get away from the water. Each of the houses sport a single large letter on one side, and seem empty. Some sort of rental cabins, all the way out here. Can't escape it.

As I scout, staying well away from the path, I see several of the buildings connect directly to the water. These have small boats tied to wooden piers that extend, rickety and crooked, to the river.

I kill the engine, pull the duffel bag from its place on the rack, open it, and take the handgun. This goes into my pocket, heavy metal dragging my shorts half off my hips.

The bags are set down in the soil. With the hiking pole in hand, I rise and move to the pier. My wrist aches with the effort of supporting my frame.

The boat is small, an unpainted aluminum shell with a small outboard motor mounted to the rear. A chain connects it to the pier and a padlock secures the circuit.

A small wooden shed stands a few feet away; I hobble to it. Two black wasps buzz from within when I force open the door; I ignore them and peer inside.

A can of gas rests on the floor and a few garden tools hang from the walls. Something skitters in the corner when the light reaches it.

No key.

"What the hell are you doing?"

I step back and turn to my left. An older man stands, fists clenched, a few feet behind me. He is taller than me, and stout, white beard covering his neck and cheeks.

My reaction is automatic; my hand dives to my pocket and retrieves the gun, which I level at his chest.

"Stand over there," I tell him, motioning with the pistol toward the grass, closer to his house. "I need the key to that boat and then I'll leave you alone."

The man doesn't move. His eyes shoot from my face to my hand, and he stares at the weapon for a second, dumbfounded. Then his eyes travel back to my face, startled mind realizing I am indeed a person, and am indeed pointing a revolver at him.

"Okay," the man says, thick white beard parting to release the words. "Okay, don't do nothing stupid."

"The key," I say, raising the gun from his chest to the center of his head. "Where is it?"

"Whoa, now," he says. "The key's over here, on the boat." He points at the little aluminum frame.

The pier is narrow, and I want to keep distance between us. I hobble to the side, stepping off the pier slowly, hiking pole leading my way.

"You get it," I tell him.

My hostage walks haltingly down the pier, then bends low and places a boot on the boat. It shifts in the water, knocking against the wood. He reaches under the single metal bench and pulls a small key and thin black magnet from its hiding place. When the two are separated he presents the key, held between stubby fingers.

"Walk back across," I say. "Stand over here."

He returns, taking slow steps across the pier. The man sweats, face red, lips moving as he mutters silently. He leans forward, keeping his distance, and drops the key into my hand.

"What's your name?" I ask.

"Tom," he answers quickly, attempt at a pleasant inflection warped by the tension in his voice. "What's your name?"

"Don't have one," I say. "Tom, I'm going to take this boat into that water, and I'll be out of your hair forever. Just don't move for a minute."

I step backward, glancing back at the duffel bag, then at my captive. When I reach the bag, I drop the walking stick and lower myself to one knee. I keep the bag's contents out of view as I open the zipper halfway and stick my hand inside.

I don't count, only pinch off a little stack of hundreds. The bills are curled from the humidity, and the paper is soft in my hand, crispness gone.

When the bag is sealed and I'm a few steps closer to him, I speak. "Take this money. This is for getting a gun pointed at you—I know, it sucks. Then I want you to stand over there, about twenty feet away, for a few minutes while I get the boat started. I'll be able to see if you run. Once I'm gone, you can do whatever you want, okay? But it'd make me real happy if you didn't call the cops."

He remains still.

"Come on," I say. "I insist." I stretch out my hand and shake the bills at him.

Tom walks forward slowly, eyes still on the pistol in my hand. He reaches out and takes the money then shuffles back, fingers clutching the little stack of hundreds as he moves. When he's returned to his original position, he turns to face me and nods.

"Okay," he says. "I'll stand here. This good?"

"That's fine. I'm going to put this gun in my pocket so I can move my things. But, the safety is off, and it's ready to go, so don't come running down here."

"I'm not," he says. "I swear."

I stay on the pier while I work the key into the padlock, twisting hard to release its grip. The chain slides out from the steel loop, and each link sings as it runs across the side of the boat to land in a coil inside—a terrible, alien racket against the constant sound of crickets.

The half-full can of gasoline goes in first, followed by my backpack and the duffel bag. I lower myself until I'm sitting on the pier. With my left hand, I lift my bad leg over the boat.

I drop in, hands clutching the sides to balance myself. The craft only wobbles slightly, pitching against the pier and bouncing back. I scoot on hands and feet to the rear of the vessel, and eye the motor. I prime it, then tug the ripcord.

It whines to life, engine sputtering. The twist of a lever pushes me a few feet forward, and I turn the rudder to guide myself deeper into the water.

When I turn back to look, Tom has vanished. I take this as a sign and increase my speed; the nose tilts upward as I propel myself further into the swamp.

47. Glimmer

I GLIDE FORWARD into a new world. All sense of direction is lost; only the winding rivers guide me. I opt for increasingly wide channels, hoping the streams converge as they near the gulf.

A snake weaves its way along the surface of the water, body undulating in primal rhythms. It moves close to my boat and I could reach out and touch it, if I tried.

I don't.

The police must be closer, now. Soon enough, they'll know I stole this boat, and then they'll know where I set off from.

They might be searching, but the swamp is a big place. I decide to try stealth, and a few miles into my journey I kill the engine. I float on gently, cutting a path through the murky green.

On occasion, I spot an alligator resting on the shore, or see something in the water that might be a log—but maybe not. More unnerving is the sound of splashing ahead of me, as creatures with senses more keen than mine clear a path.

Morgan's duffel bag sits in one corner of the boat, little beads of moisture collating on the black canvas surface. The object of everyone's attention, sitting sullen in the corner—reduced to an unwieldy burden in our wild new environment.

I lean forward, balancing carefully, and pick it up. The effort drags a groan from my body.

The zipper gets stuck at three different places along its track, but quick tugs break it free. The bag opens to reveal the tired, damp bills that are cramped inside.

Weird to think that Morgan is out there, somewhere, and doesn't have this with her. She always had the bag, it was a part of her. She can't have planned to leave me with it.

Makes me wonder. I dig through with both hands, lifting stacks of bills, letting them fall back inside. The smartphone, a black rectangle that's all screen, rests unused—haven't seen it since Jack used it as a map after Lake Charles. Two revolvers hang heavy in the corner, each loaded with the safety on.

In the back, a black tube. Thought it was a flashlight, at first—but it's just a plastic cylinder. I grab it; it's warm with the day.

The tube comes out of the bag and I twist the top half. It begins to unscrew, resisting first, then sliding easily as threads guide it through the rotation.

Inside: a plastic bag and a letter. Below that, a cell phone.

Now, this is curious.

I fish out the plastic bag, first. There is something metal inside, and the contents are coated with a sticky brown tar.

The bag peels open, sides glued together by the muck. A rotten smell wafts up; I turn the bag upside down and a heavy piece of metal falls to the floor of the boat with a knock.

It's a folding knife, a big one. Maybe five inches of handle, so another five of blade if it were opened.

The tar, then, might be dried blood. I let the weapon sit and pull the letter out next.

Two small paragraphs are typed out at the center of the page:

Jack Vickery—real name Justin Savarin—used this knife to murder Kayla McPherson in Port Lavaca, Texas. He has a tattoo that reads 'freedom from myself' on his left arm. Both his blood and her blood should show up in a DNA test. The enclosed cell phone belonged to Kayla for the days preceding her murder, and the texts confirm my statement.

If you find this, it is because he betrayed me.

Morgan's insurance over Jack. Maybe her price for helping him hide the body—she took the murder weapon. A short leash.

Unable to resist, I turn the cylinder the rest of the way over. A small black cell phone slides out, lands in my lap. The same phone Kayla wouldn't look up from the morning this all began.

I open the clamshell phone and press the power button. But, nothing happens.

I hold my thumb down again, but again, nothing.

Shame. Would love to know what Jack and Kayla talked about.

Something occurs to me: this phone is familiar. Either Jack or Morgan purchased this one as well as the phone in my pocket. I retrieve it, and a quick check confirms they're the same model. I slide the battery pack off, then do the same with Kayla's phone, and place mine in it.

The phone powers on. I click through the simple menu system, heading to 'messages.'

Only one person texted her, and there are no names or contacts. The first exchange gives Morgan her leverage:

—Hello.

Who is this?

—This is your new life speaking. You can call me Jack.

The texts cover a few weeks—some sparse, disjointed back-and-forth, one telling the other they've arrived, and so on. I scroll to the end, to the morning she was killed:

Are you ready for me?

—I'm waiting.

This is it.

—This is it. You do everything like I said?

Almost. I put the drain plugs in Sean's closet.

—What? Why? Don't do that.

It's better this way.

—It's not better. Your dad gets the money if you're murdered. We only get it if you drown.

All you care about is money. The whole town will be talking about me. When I come back, it will blow their minds.

—You know you can't come back. You told me you were okay with that. This is forever.

I'm coming, get ready.

There are no more messages. I close the phone.

Kayla is the one who framed me, not Jack.

"When I come back."

Stupid, selfish girl.

48. The American tourist

REVELATIONS UNFOLD slow as I drift downstream, staring blankly ahead. Something Kayla said at the start of it all comes back to me, takes on new meaning. Her last words, in fact.

"You guys are going to miss me so much. See you at my funeral."

She thought she'd come back—like it was all some wonderful game. I wouldn't get the death penalty, because we'd all learn she never died in the first place. It was no problem to frame me.

But, it's not a game to Jack and Morgan.

Stupid, selfish girl. She was trying to play Jack, make the whole city into her stage. Just what an attention-starved girl, fresh out of high school and no longer the center of attention needs: to be on everyone's mind.

How would you have done it, Kayla? Jump out of your own casket at the funeral?

And I had a crush on her, once. So blind. I held her death like a torch against Jack, proof he was a psychopath. Kayla's naivety made her just as crazy as him, though. They deserve each other.

Jack stood to lose a lot, without much gain. Except, maybe the bag of money she carried across the gulf, the money she borrowed as paycheck and credit card loans.

What was it Jack told me? 'Kayla didn't know the value of a dollar.'

And if Kayla's body never came to light, it all may have been saved. Morgan convinced me she'd driven away, and the police may have accepted the idea she drowned.

Even in death, Kayla wouldn't stick to the plan. The body was found.

And, what about Morgan? The murder weapon has been here all along. Could have shown it to the police, could have freed me.

I've played that game of Xs and Os, though. No one can turn Jack in without facing retribution.

And they never told me what Kayla did. I guess it was kinder to just let me think Jack was responsible. Morgan's doing, surely. All the times Jack might have told me, and she jumped into the conversation to cut him off.

I take the plastic bag, heavy with Jack and Kayla's combined blood, and carefully pick the knife up from the floor of the boat—making certain not to put my fingerprints on it. I switch the batteries out of Kayla's phone and return everything to the cylinder the way I found it. Morgan's protection against Jack goes back in the bag.

Somewhere in the distance, dogs bark, breaking my trance. Is it the bark of a bloodhound, tracking me? The old man probably told the police about his boat; they could be close.

Torn between turning the engine on and running for it, or sticking with stealth. I watch as the channel of water narrows, widens, and intersects with others. With my camouflage shirt and dull gray boat, I opt for silence, drifting along with senses on alert.

Occasionally, buried deep within the volume of the crickets, I think I hear the crackle of a radio. But, the dense barrage of sounds from the swamp make me question my own hearing—not sure if I can trust myself.

Then I catch the sound of the dread predator: the unmistakable chop of helicopter blades. The noise doubles in volume every few seconds, coming from behind. I direct the boat to the bank, underneath a particularly expansive tree, and clutch its roots with one hand. Leaves shelter me, broad scales the size of my hand.

The blades buffer the air for what seems impossibly long; first coming from the behind, then ahead, then seemingly from every direction equally. Eventually, though, as my hand cramps from holding against the constant pull of the current, the noise fades. I let go and continue my journey.

They're near.

Ahead, I spot a strange nook in the water. The channel bends but the outside edge is distended, creating a small cove. The cove is brimming with trash: a broken hot water heater, a plastic tarp, and large plates of dulled metal. The flow of the river drags me toward the refuse, and my boat will join the sad heap soon. Some naturally gathered dump, drawn here by a quirk in the current.

I tug the drawstring and the motor putters to life; I accelerate gently, pushing myself away from the nook and into the clear water. As I float away, though, I turn and examine the trash.

Something rounded and metal is jutting from the water, forced upright by the current, bobbing as water wafts through. It looks suspiciously like the top half of a metal canoe.

A canoe. Ideas rush unbeckoned, formless and nameless. Not a proper plan, but something. An inkling, the barest seed of a strategy.

I reach for a root, grab it, and pull with my whole body. With my good leg hitched around the bench where I rest, I bring the boat behind a shallow outcropping, on the same bit of land with the garbage. I toss the duffel bag and hiking cane to the shore, then my backpack, then crawl up—one foot dipping into the water as I pull myself on hands and elbows over the mud. I turn back and pull the boat halfway on the land with me, straining with both hands, upper body slick with sweat.

My landing place is a long, narrow strip of hard mud, and I see another stream about twenty feet away. The outcropping is surrounded by flowing water, but a half-dozen trees guard it from above.

I stop, resting on the cool ground. There is evidence in my boat that would go a long way to convincing the police I didn't kill Kayla. I could turn myself in, now, and put my fate in their hands. It could work, conceivably, once they heard my entire story.

But I don't want to. It would put Morgan in danger. Morgan, the only person to actually help me through any of this. And they'd take her money, as well.

Mostly, though, I don't want to be Sean Reilly again. I try to picture school, home, a career. I can't.

Everyone thinks I'm dead, and that's okay. I was scared of the void, of the loneliness, at first—but there's a peace in the nothing.

I've let go, now. Sometime in the truck, after Morgan's arrest, it all fell away. To be a ghost.

I rise. Something dull and brown moves at one end of the peninsula. I stand, hiking pole ready, and hobble a few feet over.

Three alligators, each longer than I am tall, rest on the bank just a few yards away. If they see me, they register nothing, and only sit sedate in a small patch of fading sunlight.

I freeze when I imagine I hear the helicopter again. Something is buzzing, something far in the distance. The mechanical scream is higher pitched, though, and the direction is different.

It's not a helicopter this time, I realize. It's a boat, somewhere nearby. They've nearly found me.

49. Once more into the gulf

I STARE DOWN AT THE PIT of jagged metal trash, knowing that if I fall in, I will not be able to swim out. One slip and I'll drown there, pinned between someone's rusting grill pit and an empty metal barrel that once contained industrial waste.

The stagnant green water brims with the same industry that infected Port Lavaca: buckets, hubcaps, rotors and axles. Plastic and metal that don't belong. My body is suspended over it all, supported by my hand wrapped around a thick tree branch.

My free arm is extended, hiking pole in hand, poking through the refuse. I push away a trash can, then try to force what looks like part of a lawn mower aside, but it's stuck in the mud.

The tree branch supporting me creaks; I tighten every muscle, dreading the fall, holding my breath.

It doesn't come. The branch holds. I reach further out, tip of my walking stick catching on the object of my desire. I pull, and it moves a little.

With the hiking pole hooked on the large aluminum shell, I pull us both toward the bank. The wet hull juts up from the swamp like some long-forgotten alien monument. It holds water, and it takes all my strength to tug it a few inches nearer.

My good leg pushes into the soft mud, body strained as the bent little aluminum boat comes ashore. I tip it over and brown water splashes out, black, inch-long fish drained back into the swamp.

The little craft is twisted in its center, bent up around itself. When I turn it upside down, I can clearly see the crease in the metal.

I kneel, put both hands on the bend and push. It bends a bit; I push harder, with all my weight pressed into my two hands. The metal gives slightly, bulging crease evening out. I push again, then again, like I'm giving CPR. The aluminum is slick with muck, but otherwise firm.

Working the cold, wet metal leaves me breathless, but as I collapse down on its frame, I see many of the creases are straightened. I can't spot any leaks.

A sound bites at my ears: the hum of a motor boat, somewhere in the distance. Close enough that I can make out the whine of the engine as it revs. The same boat as before, or a new one?

I take a moment to walk halfway across the peninsula, and see my reptilian neighbors still relax in the last remnants of sun.

When I reach my things, I open the backpack and retrieve a hunting knife I bought at the outdoor supply store. Then I bend to the duffel bag and pull out the pistol Morgan bought me. I tuck this into the waist of my shorts.

I spread my sleeping bag over the ground, setting my flashlight next to it. Then I crawl into the bag, roll from side to side, and climb back out. With one hand holding the backpack open, I pull items from it at random—snacks, the jug of water, and a newspaper I snatched on the way out the store. When I'm finished with the camp, I take a step back and observe. It looks like I've slept here, or intended to.

Now, the hard part.

The hunting knife is in my hand, tip directed at my chest.

I can do this. I am not Sean Reilly—I am that which crawled out of the gulf.

Can't do it; my head starts to spin, so I lower myself to the dirt, legs stretched out ahead. Deep breaths settle my nerves. The blade glints in the light, surface flawless and new, singing the yellow hues of the sunset.

I turn the tip toward my right shoulder, then bring the knife close. I hold my breath, remember why I am here, and slash the metal across my shirt and skin.

My movement is a quick jerk, a slicing motion that splits flesh. Breath exhales in a ragged hiss as the stinging pain slowly registers. Blood emerges, purple on my camo shirt, and begins to run freely from the shallow cut.

The blade turns to my stomach. I make another cut here, hissing, pain not as shocking this time. My wet sera stains my shirt again, running down my abs and pooling where my shorts hold tight to my hips.

Then my right arm. I sit back for a moment, leaning to the ground, head spinning from the sight of blood pouring from me. I fall back, curling into a fetal position, making little stabs into my arm. The cuts are deep enough, a half-inch or more, and blood wells up from the patterns and stains my clothes. Must be fast, before my appetite for it fades.

Literal self-destruction. I continue the pseudocide, marking myself with a slice on the thigh of my injured leg, fevered creature rolling in the mud. The pain washes up like a beached wave, and I go light-headed, close my eyes. A brutal, raw itch from every wound. My clothes soak with blood as the cuts pulse.

I turn my attention to my cast. The black plastic is drenched with sweat, blood and mud. The smell is rotten. Two screws connect the joints where the cast links my thigh and shin; I work the tip of the knife into these screws and twist, gradually unscrewing them, only stopping to wipe blood from my slick fingers.

Dreading this. When the screws are cleared, the cast comes apart, two halves losing their bond. My body knows the pain of my knee well—those pathways are worn smooth with use, and the hurt rushes through as I relax my naked knee onto the ground.

To unmake oneself.

The shoes are next—laces wet and slick with mud. It takes me ages to work the knot free with shaking fingers. Then they're off, and the socks go in them.

After I take the gun from my shorts and put it on the ground next to me, I unbutton them. They fall, violet with blood. The boxers next; I thread my broken knee through carefully, and soon my bare ass is pressed into the ground. Moments later, the shorts are joined by my shirt.

The whole bloody pile of clothes sit in a grim, wet wad. The only other article of clothing I own—a pair of black nylon rain pants—is pulled from the backpack and slid over my legs, covering me.

I look up, distracted by the sound of air being pulverized by helicopter blades. Can't locate anything through the trees, though I hear it clearly. Somewhere behind that, I think a dog is barking.

Must move fast. With one hand on the gun and another on the walking stick, I crawl clumsily toward the alligators on hands and knee, stopping every yard to pull the pile of clothes along with me. My bad leg drags behind, mud clinging to my ankle. Once I climb over a patch of dried weeds that dig into my palms, I'm within range.

The reptiles still sit motionless, ancient eyes watching a world millions of year younger than my own. Even when I am five feet away, they show no sign of registering my intrusion.

Then, I pick up my bloody shirt and throw it at them. It arcs through the air and lands with a soft plop between two of the beasts, fabric stretching across one gator's clawed paw.

But, they don't move. I follow up with the bloodstained shorts, aiming for the head of the biggest. This lands perfectly, covering the eyes of the animal, who jerks to the side with a hiss.

The animals come alive, rising from their rest and elevating on four squat limbs, ready. Jaws snap closed around the offending fabric—once, twice, then they're left on the dirt.

All three crocodiles scamper with ferocious speed, turning to face me. I rise carefully, lifting myself with my good leg and walking stick, pistol in my other hand.

I face a chorus of hissing reptiles. Jaws open, teeth bared, dozens of gleaming white daggers displayed. I lean forward carefully, weight on the pole, and pick up my shoe. I toss this into the open mouth of the alligator furthest to the left, whose jaws snap around it for a moment before dropping the bit of plastic and leather.

One of the long lizards rockets forward, arms and legs akimbo, and in three strides the raw bones of his teeth glint as jaws snap at my foot—I jerk back, hiking pole flailing, backpedaling twice, but it follows, biting at my broken leg in primeval rage, missing by inches. I throw myself backward, falling to the ground, leaving a bloody print in the dirt.

The gun is in my hand, aimed at the gator who hunches motionless only a few feet away, mouth open in defiance. It doesn't advance; my finger is tight on the trigger. Slowly I stand, pulse pounding, breath coming in ragged gasps.

I lean toward my remaining possessions, grabbing my disassembled cast. The reptile twitches, long tail sweeping aside leaves in the dirt, body shifting, trained on my every motion.

I toss the cast at its face, underhanded. This brings more hissing, a flurry of dust—the jaw snaps twice around the plastic, which explodes in a shower of black fragments.

My second shoe follows, bouncing harmlessly from its body, unnoticed. Last, I stab the boxers with my hiking pole, then jab it toward the animal. Jaws snap around the aluminum staff, wrenching it from my grip instantly, thousand pounds of force clamping down. The maw shuts over the pole and attached fabric, and clear dents are left in the metal.

The animal advances again, a foot closer. I pull myself back, scampering through mud that sticks to my open wounds, putting distance between myself and the gators.

I crawl to Morgan's duffel bag and slide the strap over my bleeding shoulder. I turn and watch wide-eyed to see what they do, but nothing followed me to the campsite.

I spread out on my two elbows and one good knee and crawl to the little aluminum craft I pulled from the garbage heap. My raw skin scrapes against the filthy metal; blood stains everything I touch. I drag my torso up and over the edge, then push with my good leg, shoving the muddy bank away. When I'm floating, I pull myself inside and curl into a fetal position, where I close my eyes and quietly bleed.

50. Of ghosts and shadows

THE BASIN WITHIN MY BOAT is lined with my blood; it stains the grooves of the warped metal. A womb to carry me, or an altar where I'm sacrificed, but really both.

As I float downstream, two helicopters converge, heading back up the river. They hover over my little peninsula, the scene of my latest staged death. Lights beam down into the tree cover, searching.

I think they've found the scene I left them. Can only hope my distraction buys time, lets me slip away. The blood, the boat, my gear—I hope it's enough to fool them. Never know.

The current, at least, welcomes me. It carries me toward the gulf, boat bouncing from rocks and roots and tumbling along toward the ocean. A vulture circles overhead, riding drafts in lazy arcs, soaring through the evening sky.

I don't move; only lay, bare back pressed into the rough ridges of the ruined aluminum tub that holds me. The peculiar creases in its base, the same ones I worked so hard to straighten earlier, press into my spine.

Calling it a boat is generous. The misshapen hull rocks wildly to one side or the other any time I shift my weight. To stay afloat, I spread across all corners of the tub and balance carefully.

But, I am moving. The clouds attest to that, thick and gray as they tumble by, promising rain. With the sky blotted, the sunset begins to burn away in gasping shades of pink, green and purple.

Morgan's bag rests beside my head. I lift an arm, muscles aching, and unzip it. I feel around blindly, brushing past money and guns, until I grip something smooth and rectangular.

The smartphone. There are only two buttons to press; I hold each down for a few seconds until the screen comes to life.

One bar of battery, no signal. I toss the phone into the bag, zip it all closed again, and let my arm fall. Whatever good that will do.

I watch my hand, pressed to the side of the boat. The shadow between myself and the hull dissolves slowly, pressed under my body and draining away as the light fails.

What was it Kayla told me? Night is when our shadows talk.

I didn't understand it then, but I might now.

Ghosts and shadows—the private and public person. Well, I am all ghost now, happy to hover over Sean Reilly's dead image.

Feels like liberty.

Night falls. The cold and the dark seem to soothe my cuts, and the bleeding stops. I am weak, though, and light-headed. Not sure I could rise if I wanted. I am spent.

<hr/>

Sometime in the middle of the night, the boat begins to rock more fervently. What were once occasional disturbances become a constant, rhythmic pulse.

Head pounding, mouth dry. My hands cling to the rim of the tub on opposite sides; I pull myself upright.

I go all dizzy. I assume my vision is spinning, and yet the world is such flawless dark that I couldn't know. The sense of tossing about in the boat is my only clue the situation has changed. Otherwise, the sounds tell me nothing. The slap of the hull on water, the rush of wind passing my ears—and a ravenous, all-devouring blackness.

Is this death?

My back presses to the boat once more as I collapse. I float through nothing.

One last deconstruction. Destroy Sean Reilly the shadow, then destroy the body, and now the world is stolen from my eyes.

I breathe in. Salted air courses past my lips, into my lungs. Membranes cleave free oxygen, universal fuel that burns in us all, and I exhale. There is always breath.

Don't even need to count them, anymore.

51. In peace there's nothing

MORNING COMES SLOW.
What should be neon radiance is dull and muted, thick clouds swathing the morning sky. Celestial gauze.

Slowly, I pull myself upright, careful not to upset my balance. Dried blood stains the boat in brown-red rivers, congealing in a sunken corner.

The sunrise doesn't come. In this dim light, the water is the same color as the sky, and there's no line between the two. It feels like the whole thing wraps around me, heaven and sea, like a tunnel. Like the boat could surge forward, tumble into the horizon.

I'm not seeing any land, I realize. That means in the night, I drifted past the beach where I was supposed to meet Morgan. Could be miles from shore.

So, I'm doomed.

But, something catches my attention—a thin sliver of substance creeping in from the right edge of my vision. The little craft must be spinning slightly. Slowly, the threshold of the earth creeps past. This wedge of land cuts across the dull gray.

The beach is closer than I dared to hope, maybe a mile away. I could tip myself, try to swim. But, I can barely sit up straight; can't fight hundreds of yards of current.

So I lean back in the tub and lie still.

There is still the phone, if it has life left. If it finds a connection. If Morgan is watching, waiting to track it.

But mostly, there is nothing to do but wait and die.

A sudden warmth overcomes me. My mind empties, and my breathing comes easier. The peace that's been with me since I gave up in the truck returns, stronger now.

I smile. With my mind emptied, my focus turns to what's happening around me. Can feel the sea spray drift across my skin, each droplet activating a nerve. The sensation is incredible. The raw hurt of my cuts dull to a soft itch. Each pitch and roll of the boat cradles me, bringing soft thrills as I dip and dive.

I close my eyes, smile, and relax. Going to enjoy what life is left. Maybe for the first time.

For the first time, completely alone and totally free. Can't have one without the other, I think. The world sees me as dead, and there's no reason to tell them otherwise.

I sleep for hours, awakened only by the fall of warm rain across my face. The same peaceful calm fills my limbs, clears my head. If this is death, it isn't so bad.

But where there was nothing, there is now something. So small a difference that I cannot pinpoint it exactly. I stretch my focus to my ears, picking each sound apart: the waves in the distance, the water under the craft. Rain falling against metal, rain falling against my skin. There is something else. Can't hear it, not yet, but I feel it.

A deep rumble. I turn my head, press an ear into the metal, feel the dry blood against my cheek. There it is.

A motor. I hear a motor.

Both hands grip the edges, pull. Tired, malnourished muscles like frayed ropes ache as they tighten, tearing against one another. The base of my neck protests in pain as it supports a pounding skull.

Less than a hundred yards away is a cream colored fiberglass boat, maybe fifteen feet tall. Nose high in the air; small, calm waves broken under it. I lift a hand into the air, wave.

It nears, roar muted as the engine is hushed, then silenced, and the vessel floats gently next to me, now only a couple of yards away. Being near the larger boat sets mine on edge, sending me sliding wildly along the water.

A coil of smooth black rope flies into view, tossed from the craft. It lands silently in the sea nearby. A pale face looks over the edge.

"You look like hell," Morgan says.

I smile.

Made in the
USA
Monee, IL

15139637R00116